THE
DESPERATE
SEARCH

THE
DESPERATE
SEARCH

By
ARTHUR MAYSE

Sears Readers Club
Chicago · 1952

This is a special edition published exclusively for the members
of SEARS READERS CLUB, P. O. Box 6570A, Chicago 80,
Illinois. It was originally published by WILLIAM MORROW
& COMPANY.

THE
DESPERATE
SEARCH

VINCE ARDAGH, IN HIS RESTLESS PROWLING, DISCOVERED A loose patch on the seaplane's portside float. That gave him something to do beside chain-smoke and worry about the weather, and he tackled the repair job gratefully, cutting a new plate from sheet dural, drilling it and securing it with a collar of rivets. He was still on his knees by the Viking, trouble lamp looped around his neck, when he heard Tagish whine from the mouth of the hangar.

A full moon was bad medicine for some dogs, but it was fog the lank black-and-tan Doberman hated. Tagish could have been a pilot himself, the way fog bothered him. Ardagh called, and the dog came with a quiet padding to stand by his shoulder.

"Me neither," Ardagh told him softly. "But it's only a ground mist this time. Let's not be fools about it, eh?"

Talking to Tagish was one of the quirks Nora Stead had done her best to iron out of him, back in that other existence when Nora was his wife. She had never fully succeeded, and in the eighteen months since their crack-up he had resumed the habit. He and the Dober-

1

man were tested friends, much alone, and there are times when a lonely man badly needs escape from the prison of his brain.

"Look now. They've got ground-controlled approach, haven't they?" He rocked off his heels, the trouble light thumping his chest, his shadow lengthening enormously across the concrete floor. "Two gets you twenty they set her down without even waking 'em."

Tagish whined again, deep in his throat, and Ardagh dropped a hand to the prick-eared head.

"Darn if I didn't forget to tell you," he said. "I've got news for you. Big news, mister. Our kids are coming home. Don and Janet, you remember them?"

Six months, which can be a long enough time in a man's life, is very much longer in a dog's. But a grin woke in the steady amber eyes that quested the bush pilot's face. Against his knee he felt a responsive thrill, the tremor which in a less dignified beast would have signified the wagging of a tail. Tagish had been Don's dog, and always would be. The question was an insult to his intelligence. Sure, Tagish remembered.

The office side door was open. Eight-thirty, the wall clock said—half an hour to go, if Coastwise-Pacific's Flight Three from Los Angeles was on time. There were no more odd jobs worth doing, and Ardagh's restlessness demanded action.

"Come on," he said. "We can sweat them in better with a cup of coffee."

He ran the hangar doors back a squeaking yard on their rollers. They stepped out to a blind gray world. Ardagh, feeling in his chest the claustrophobic tightness

2

which fog always brought him, realized the full meaning of the Doberman's unease. The ground mist of an hour ago had thickened into a murk that lay solid on river and sea and the flatlands between. It was late in the season for a pea-souper, but June had been a queer month even for the British Columbia coast, the weather chopping and changing from day to day. They wouldn't be in. Only a lunatic or a cripple would try for a landing in this.

Disappointment stabbed him, and a targetless anger. Another bollix. Standing above the seaplane ramp, the suck and gurgle of the river in his ears, he thought yearningly of the bottle in his desk.

Somewhere along the line, his luck had played out. It had been dripping like antifreeze from a leaky radiator while he was still all ambition and dewy hope, the hot pilot who stayed home nights with his family, the smart operator who sank twenty thousand bucks in the setup which was to make him rich. Upcoast Airways. A secondhand ship and a mess of thirdhand gear, a tumbledown hangar and a grudging green light from the Canadian Department of Transport. He'd been going to change all that. If Nora had stuck with him, they might have. But when Nora's break came she had taken it, and to hell with anything or anyone in her way.

He turned his back on the sullen river. Ceiling might lift—there was always the outside chance—and the bottle would keep.

Walking slowly, the big dog at his side, he cut across toward the Municipal Airport limits. On the invisible highway he heard a car grope by in second gear. The airport beacon revealed itself only in a spaced lightening

3

overhead. Don and Janet wouldn't come tonight. It was just wishful thinking that impelled him, and selfish thinking at that. Flight Three would be diverted to Seattle. The children would be well looked after, of course, but even so, they were young for traveling alone.

He thought of Nora again, with a resentment that shook and hurt. She should have brought them. She could have taken that much time off without putting a crimp in her precious career.

His heels echoed loud in the deserted waiting room as he passed through to the coffee bar. A girl sat at the far end, a black-haired girl in a blue trench coat, the collar turned up. He straddled the stool next her; Tagish settled between them with a faint grating of claws on linoleum.

The smile the girl gave him was friendly and tired. "Don't you ever go home, Vince?"

"Might as well, I suppose. The gulls will be afoot by morning."

Her name was Julia Thorne, and she covered the airport for the *Telegram*. These last few months, partly because she was the only reporter who still kept regular tab on Upcoast Airways, he had taken to feeding her what scraps of news came his way. A good kid, no glamour girl, so much in love with her job it was funny, but not at all ambitious. He'd known one glamour girl with ambitions. One was plenty.

She hadn't been in long. Fog moisture still glistened on her short, straight hair. Ardagh suspected why she was here. Now she confirmed it.

"We heard Nora Stead might arrive tonight. If she did and I missed her, they'd kick me back to social."

4

"You're safe," Ardagh told her. "Flight Three won't make it. Anyway, Nora wasn't coming."

"Just the children?"

"Yeah." He had never talked about the kids to her, but she'd know. The divorce had been well publicized. "Nora's busy. Up to her ears in a new picture, I see by your paper."

"Still . . ."

Jule Thorne let it hang there, and he said in automatic defense, "There was no point in her coming. Kids travel pretty young these days."

"I know. Trans-Canada had twins from Scotland last week. Four years old. How old are yours now?"

"Eight years and going on three." The counterman poured him coffee and Ardagh reached for his cigarettes. "Take it easy or I'll be showing you my pictures."

"Why not? I'd like to see them."

Trying to give him a lift. Gloom must stick out all over him. But he dug for his wallet, pleased in a foolish sort of way, and with some of the night's raw chill draining from him.

There were half a dozen snapshots, all from the last Christmas visit. He shucked out the one he liked best—Janet in her play pen, Don leaning over the rail with the proprietary air he always showed toward his sister, while Tagish sat gravely watchful in the background. That was the morning a strange dog ventured into the yard. The Doberman had all but killed him.

"A blondy," Jule said. "He takes after you." The smile was in her gray eyes as well as on her lips. "His sister will envy him that hair when she's sixteen."

"Janet's hair is nice enough. Brown, like her mother's. Kind of curly."

"Nora Stead's is auburn these days," Jule said lightly. "You ought to keep up with the times, Vince."

She returned the snap. "How long do you have them with you?"

"Till school opening."

Eleven weeks, taking it from tomorrow. Seventy-seven days and nights, and he grudged even a night of it. He wasn't going to think beyond their visit. It was like when you were a youngster yourself, with summer vacation stretching ahead. You couldn't see to the end. You wouldn't let yourself see.

"I suppose you'd bite my head off if I asked to borrow them one day? Take them downtown or to the beach or somewhere?" Her face was for the moment wistful, and he realized the dark girl was older than he had thought. Jule added hastily, "Just for fun, I mean, sometime when you're out on a charter. Not for a story."

"Thanks. They'd get a bang out of that." Mrs. Urquhart was good with them, trustworthy and kind, even if she did scare hell out of Don with her yarns of kelpies and such. But children need someone young. Someone like Jule Thorne might keep Don and Janet happy.

"I will, then. It's a promise." Jule pushed back her sleeve and glanced at her watch. "No announcement about Flight Three yet. I expected we'd have it by now."

"It'll come," Ardagh said. Tagish was snoring gently at their feet. The clock's ticking intruded itself upon them, and the clink of dishes out back. By the blind look of the

windows he knew the fog had not lifted. He realized too
that the tension which he had shed for a while was building in him steadily again.

He got up, stretching his arms and wriggling his shoulders in the scuffed leather jacket. "Wouldn't hurt to call
the tower. They may know something."

"I'll check with Coastwise-Pacific," Jule said, and passed
him, square-shouldered in her belted coat, a slim girl with
nice legs, nothing of Nora's studied grace about her, but
confidence and a quality which might be pride.

He had hoped to get Hopkins or someone he knew, but
the voice that passed him the traffic report belonged to
a stranger. Flight Three of Coastwise-Pacific Airlines, it
told him briskly, had last made radio contact at eight-
thirty-eight, when the captain had announced his intention of turning back to his alternate port. Nothing there
to get spooked up about. It was a natural decision—the
inevitable decision for a trained and careful officer. Next
to the bush pilots, no one knew the fog belt better than
the Coastwise-Pacific crowd.

Ardagh trusted the air. It had given him his living for
fifteen of his thirty-one years. He had fought a war in it
and emerged with no more damage than a flak scar down
where it didn't show. As a bush pilot ferrying passengers
and freight wherever a charter might take him, he had
logged more hours than many of the seniors on the main-
stem lines. But his trust was a personal one, calling for
his own hands on the wheel, his feet on the pedals, his
personal judgment opposed to the treacheries of air and
weather. Although the word from the tower had been
plain enough, it failed to ease the tautness of his nerves.

7

His marriage had turned out a bust. By October, unless more charters slipped through the efficient cordon of the big lines, Upcoast Airways would have folded. All he had left were his daughter and his son.

Hands shoved deep into his pockets, he returned to his stool. He waited, an unlighted cigarette between his lips, until Jule Thorne came back from the information desk phone.

"Heading for Seattle," he told her. "I don't know why those monkeys didn't put it on the P.A. It would have saved us a wait."

Something in the girl's face puzzled him. A stiffness, a forced quality to her smile that weariness alone couldn't account for. He said sharply, staring at her, "You holding out on me? You pick up something?"

"No . . . No, not a thing." She sat down beside him and took a cigarette from the pack by her cup. "They hung up on me, that's all. I'm good and mad."

"Why'd they hang up?"

"You tell me." She said it crossly, leaning to him for a light.

There was no reason to linger now, but they sat on, silent, the girl frowning at her shadowed reflection in the mirror, Ardagh looking down at his balled fist on the counter. This was to have been a big evening. Mrs. Urquhart had cleaned house and made oatmeal cookies enough for a regiment. The old lady was going to be disappointed. His thoughts drifted to the children's room, to Janet's crib by the end wall with the blue silk nightgown he had bought her spread over the rail. Don's new rock maple bed stood across the room with the

8

carrousel lamp on the table beside it. The lamp was new too.

A big evening, and like everything else, every other bloody thing since the war, it had folded on him.

His voice came out rough. "We're doing no good here. I've got a crock in my office. You want to come over for a drink?"

"No, thanks." She tried to keep it light, but that hint of strain was in her voice. "I don't think Tagish would approve. He's a stuffy sort of dog."

"Okay, okay. I wasn't propositioning you, if that's it."

"It isn't." She looked full at him. "Vince, they've never hung up on me before, and I've called lots later than this."

"Sure," Ardagh said. "I'm sorry. I always get nasty when I'm scared."

"Don't be," Jule told him. "Don't. I'm not, really. There's no need."

The counterman brought more coffee. He said, "Down the hatch, folks, then we'll lock up." He stood yawning, the Silex in his fist. Outside, a truck engine racketed into life. Another followed with a deeper coughing. A red beam swept the windows. The engine din leaped to a clamor that diminished as swiftly. The jangle of the phone alongside the cash register rang an answering discord inside Ardagh's skull. He lunged for the phone, grabbing it out from under the counterman's hand.

It was Hopkins. He said rapidly, "Listen, Vince, I just came on. You were calling about Flight Three. They're bringing her in."

"Like hell they are. She turned back."

9

"We got another signal a minute ago. Seattle's plugged solid."

"How about Pat Bay?"

"Intermittent clearing. But he has to get down, fast. One engine's out."

"Fire?" He shot the question harshly. His palms had begun to sweat.

"Yes."

"You can still talk him down."

"We'll try. We—"

It ended with the clang of a receiver socked hard into the cradle.

Ardagh turned. Jule Thorne, very pale, was close behind him. Her lips parted but no words emerged. Together, Tagish a following shadow, they went out to the night and the swirling fog.

Beyond the passenger gates, an airport cop was buttoning his tunic while he peered across the field. The cop pivoted with a loud "No you don't!" but Ardagh shouldered him aside and plunged on through.

The tarmac of the parking apron was under his feet. A jeep, skidding close around the tail of a North Star, squealed its brakes at him. Someone, John Brandreth, yelled, "Hey, Captain!" and he swung on board. He had forgotten the girl—forgotten everything except the senseless compulsion to get out there—but Jule Thorne cried to him now, and he grabbed her wrists and tumbled her in beside him. Across by the long south runway, headlights cut the fog in a stationary huddle.

The jeep braked, and he jumped overside. This picture was familiar in each detail—the G.C.A. radar truck, the crash wagon and ambulance, the mutter of idling motors and the sight of a man struggling into an asbestos suit. What had changed was his own place in the picture. For the first time he was not the objective onlooker, the tough professional waiting to watch other professionals pull off a dangerous landing. He was Vince Ardagh, the father of two children on whom his lonely love was centered, and they were riding a comet on its slant toward blinded earth, and nothing he could do, no skill of his could help them.

Jule's hand was on his arm. He shook it off and moved out from the jeep, his feet dragging him toward the man who waited in the asbestos crash suit, bulky and unhuman, like a lost diver's ghost.

The night loosed a new sound, no more than a humming in the blood and the brain at first, then expanding enormously, rushing down upon them from the shrouded East.

Close to Ardagh, someone said in a toneless voice, "Here she comes."

East away, a spark burned through the fog with the dull and evil red of a warrior star. The spark grew to a torch that trailed a crimson mane. Ardagh heard two voices, the same flat one saying, "What are they trying to do, talk him into the ground?" and John Brandreth's dropping calmly across it, "Shut up. They're doing all right."

Flight Three was coming in on an east-west course. By the rush of sound and the angle drawn by the torch flare, she would touch down almost level with where they stood.

Ardagh began to count, numb lips moving stiffly, and

11

had reached seven when he glimpsed substance as well as flame—the blurred whale-shape of the airliner settling toward the runway. The fire was in her portside wing root. In the instant before the pilot could pull his extinguisher, flame from the burning engine had blown back and taken hold.

She was too high. They were working, probably, in a cockpit blind with smoke; the pilot had deviated from the flight path set for him by ground control. He was coming in high, he was landing her not on the runway but in air. In a moment her wing would stall and she would loop into the field.

"Get her up." The voice was his, strained and hoarse as if his own arms fought the yoke. *"Lift her!"*

The wing did not stall. With the landing gear house-high above the strip, the pilot poured on the coal. Under her belly as she lifted, Ardagh glimpsed the ground lights on the far side of the runway, each in its nimbus of fog. The aircraft climbed as if earth rejected her, tossing her back to the sky. She thundered, rising and dwindling, into fog that closed about her like roiled water.

Someone tugged at Ardagh's sleeve. Jule Thorne was standing close to him; she offered a lighted cigarette and he took it, dragging deep, trying to clear the fog from his lungs.

"Next time around," John Brandreth said. "He'll make it next pass, Captain."

"Sure," Ardagh said. "Sure."

His mind had cleared. In that loaded second when he waited for the crash, he had gone beyond panic. The pilot up there in the soup, flying on instruments, circling

12

back to the approach range now, would have visual contact at forty feet for his next try. The fog was shifting, rolling seaward to the push of a land breeze.

"You know," Brandreth said quietly, "I believe they got their fire licked. She was down to just a glow when they hiked out."

Nothing to do but wait. Long after his cigarette was finished, he waited, keyed for the pulse beat which would swell to the growl of a homing aircraft. But that sound was not reborn, and when a star next glimmered through, its fire was a cold white spark burning a million light years away.

"He's gone to another field," Jule said. He could feel her shivering in the thin coat, and the shiver was in her voice now, too. "Vince, don't look like that. Patricia Bay may be open, or the emergency field at Saghallie. He'll land somewhere."

"Yeah," he said. The airport beacon swung its circle endlessly above them. The breeze touched his face with cold in its passing. "Somewhere."

The man in the asbestos suit was lurching toward the crash wagon. He tugged off his gauntlets and dropped them into the back of the truck.

Tagish sat a little apart, supported on spraddled forelegs, head raised as if to challenge the night. His muzzle lifted higher now, and the rumble in his taut throat fined to a noise eerie and thin as the wail of a lost child. The Doberman, the great fight-scarred dog of impregnable dignity and near-human intelligence, was pouring his soul into a howl.

THIS TIME THE RED LETTERS THAT TOLD PEOPLE THEY COULD unfasten their safety belts stayed off. Donald Ardagh tried to wish them on, but wishing didn't work, so he changed to pretending he was the Spartan boy with the live fox under his shirt. That boy was a dope, of course. He should have taken the fox out and made a pet of it instead of letting it bite him. Except he couldn't, because he was in school or something.

If he could move it would be easier. Janet sprawled heavy against him, damp and hot, with her hair tickling his face. If he moved she might wake up, though, and if Janet woke she'd be cross and almost certain to cry.

Don blew a wisp of his sister's hair away from his nose and sat stoically, a grave child eight years old and rather small for his age, fair-haired, with a double crown which had been slicked neatly flat when they boarded the plane, but now poked up in a rebel tuft. The Spartan game wasn't working very well. He gave it up presently and made himself think about landing, and Dad being there to meet them and take them home. That helped him forget how numb his arm was from Janet's limp weight, and how badly he had to go to the bathroom.

Their stewardess, the dark pretty one, came out of the pilots' compartment. Smoke oozed after her, thickening the cabin's haze. She stopped for a moment up front, and talked to a woman who cried in a high, silly voice. Then

14

she moved on along the aisle. Don said, "Hello," and she gave his hair a quick, friendly ruffle. Maybe she was scared like the other big people, but if she was it didn't show.

"How are we doing, Blondy?"

"Fine." He said it automatically. "Can I go to the bathroom now, please?"

"Pretty soon now." He and Janet already had two blankets around them, but the stewardess fetched more. She knelt and began to tuck them in, layer on layer, till they were packed in a soft but solid nest.

"We're warm enough, thanks," Don protested politely, but she wadded more blankets in around them just the same.

"It isn't that," she told him cheerfully. "I've been talking to the captain, and he says when we land we may bump."

He had been asleep when she pulled the blinds. Pulling the blinds had something to do with the trouble the plane was in. There had been the fire first, and the almost-landing. Now they flew on much as they had before the trouble started. The difference was more to be felt than put into a thought. Maybe it just came from a lot of people being scared together.

"Will it be a big bump?" Don asked the stewardess.

"Not very big, honey." Her face slipped a little, and he knew she was scared too. "Look, why don't you curl up and go to sleep?"

"I'll try," Don said. But his eyes stayed open, round and gray and questioning. He wished his father was flying this old plane.

"You still awake, boy?"

The voice, soft and deep as a low note on an organ, belonged to the bad man across the aisle.

He thought about the man, wondering if he should answer, then said, "Yes."

"Well," the man said. "Well, now!"

The other man, asleep in the window seat, was a detective. Don had seen the little chain that joined their wrists when they got on, and he knew all about handcuffs. He had a pair himself with a key to open them, at least there had been a key till Janet swallowed it. He had guns too, and a silver badge which Mr. Cassidy at the studio gates was always trying to trade for his own dull one.

"Matter of fact," the bad man said, "I been finding it a little difficult to get to sleep myself. Hit's powerful hard to sleep right, setting up this way."

You don't have anything to do with crooks and people like that. He was pretty sure, too, that Nora would be cross if she knew he'd been talking to a black man, unless he was a waiter or a porter on a train, and you were telling him to do something for you. Still, if she knew how things were in the plane, perhaps this once she wouldn't mind.

"Do you think we'll land soon?"

"Why, I 'spect so." The bad man was so black you could only see his white teeth as he grinned, and the lazy, friendly roll of his eyes. "Yes, I think we'll be down real soon now." The soft voice came closer as he shifted his weight. "You know, I been roostin' here kind of telling a story to myself. Story my daddy used to tell me when I was a li'l kid like you."

"What kind of story?" Don put the question guardedly.

16

"Sort of a bedtime story. But, shucks . . . I guess you've heard it. Your mom, she's tol' it to you and your sister many a time, I bet."

"Mother doesn't tell us stories. She hasn't got time." He puffed at Janet's hair again, and very cautiously started to free his arm. Janet twitched, and he arrested the movement. "Dad does, when we're with him. He reads me stories out of books."

"This one's 'bout a boy maybe a shade smaller than you is. Name of Apanamondas.* You ever hear tell of him, son?"

"No." It wouldn't be a big bump when they landed. Just a little one, like when you step off a curb without knowing it's there. "I guess I didn't hear his name right. The boy in the story."

" 'Panamondas." The handcuff chain glinted and vanished as the bad man settled his shoulders. He was very big, almost big enough to be a giant. "Well, now, seems this real hot day, 'Panamondas' mammy up and tells him, 'Boy, don't you be loafing round my kitchen. You just scoot 'crost de crick and pay you'se respec's to your old aunty. An' if she gives you a present, don't you be careless with it like you mos' usually is. You put it on yo' head and pull yo' hat down over it, an' walk home real careful.' "

The soft, dark voice only partly dissolved the fear that lay in a solid lump in his stomach. Fear swirled in the plane, as if it were something that had rushed in with the smoke.

* Telescoped version of story by Sarah Bryant, published 1905 and in a Houghton-Mifflin collection in 1938.

17

"So 'Panamondas, he went skippity-hop across the crick, and sure 'nuff, his old aunty give him a present, and it was a pad of yaller butter fresh out the churn. So he sets it on his head an' puts his hat on over it, and home he traipses careful as can be. And when he gets to his mammy's doorstep he whisks off his hat, an' he hollers, 'Here I is home, Mammy, with the present my aunty done give me!' But, son, what you think?"

"I don't know." He had been up lots of times with Dad, and they'd never had any trouble. Flying with Dad in the Viking last year, Tagish behind them and the seaplane trailing its shadow across the blue-green water, he hadn't been scared at all. He wasn't going to be now, either, although it would be easier if Dad were here.

"You don't know? Smart boy like you?" The velvet voice clucked softly. If the story lasted long enough, he might get to sleep. "Well, now! Like I told you, hit was a real hot day. That pad o' butter had just nat'chally melted, and there stood 'Panamondas with the butter running into his eyes and down his cheeks and off his chin. His mammy, she squawked real loud at the sight.

"''Panamondas,' she says, 'I do declare, you ain't got the sense you was bo'n with! Now next time you go to see your aunty an' she gives you a present, you set it on a burdock leaf and take that leaf an' dip it in the water an' cool it an' cool it an' coo-ool it.'"

The detective, sitting there so still with his head tipped back, hadn't been asleep after all. With a bad man to take to jail up in Canada, Don supposed he would have to stay awake.

18

"You're ahead of yourself, Albert," he said. "How about the loaf of bread?"

"Why, no suh," the black man said. "Way my daddy told it me, that loaf of bread come afterwards. Boy forgets a lot of things his folks learn him with a gad, but a story tol' in happiness, he ain't going ever to forget. So with your permission, Sergeant, I'll just tell it to this li'l fella the way I heard it."

"Okay," the detective said. "Tell him it your way, Albert."

The plane seemed to be limping in its flight, settling and staggering. Maybe they were going to try to land again. Maybe it would be only a tiny bump, not even hard enough to wake Janet.

The detective did a queer thing then. He bent and fumbled; Don heard something click. The bad man lifted his hand, the hand that had been shackled to the detective's, and flexed wrist and fingers.

"Thank you, suh," he said. "I 'preciate that."

"Better get on with your story," the detective said.

The dark velvet voice, infinitely soothing, returned to summer and the South. Don's eyes were growing sandy. He closed them, thinking drowsily, *If the story lasts just a bit longer, I'll go to sleep. When I wake up the bump will be over and Dad will be there.*

". . . So very next day, 'Panamondas goes skippity-hop across the crick, and he chops up his aunty some fatwood for her stove, an' darn if she don't give him a puppy dog all for his own . . ."

"A Doberman?" The question came in a muffled murmur. "We've got a Doberman."

"Could be. Now I recall, I think that's sure 'nuff what he was, son. So 'Panamondas, he takes that puppy dog real careful, an' sets him on a burdock leaf just like his mammy told him, and he sinks de leaf in de crick, an' he cools it . . . an' coo-ools it . . . an' coo-oo-ools it . . .' "

The plane bucked violently, lunging upward. It checked with a jar that hurled him against the back of the seat ahead, Janet hugged tight in his arms, the two of them tangled and muffled in their blanket cocoon. There was a tearing and a crashing, a scream that soared shrilly and went on and on and on. They slewed to the left and down. The plane leaped and jolted with a din that was like cannon crackers exploding in ragged sequence. Something whipped the blanket off his face. He glimpsed the tops and trunks of trees through a hole up front which was big and gaping like an open door. A black bulk thrust itself between his eyes and those racing, exploding trees. It folded him and shielded him with bent arm and thighs and muscle-padded torso. Its hand cupped his head and buried his face against a sweaty and convulsively jerking throat. Outside—inside the plane—in his own head—there was one crash louder than all the others. Then the bump came, and he dived into blackness of sleep thinking, *It was only a tiny bump, only a tiny bump after all.*

THE YOUNG INDIAN OF THE SEAHHOST BAND HAD GONE through residential school as Charles Koskima, but now he was finished with being educated, people had taken to calling him by his kid name, Chuck-Charley, again. It was good to be done with school—at least it would be if it wasn't for Grandfather Koskima. It did beat hell how Grandfather stuck by the old ways. He wouldn't talk to you in English if he could help it, and it had taken Father Jerome half a day to make him see the sense of white man's school.

This business of chasing him off upriver was another of Grandfather's stunts. It seemed in the old days a boy wasn't a man till he went out alone to the mountains and spent three days starving himself. At the end of the three days, when he was good and beat up, he looked around for some bird or animal and whatever it might be, that thing stayed his totem for the rest of his life. Then he came down and there was a lot of fancy partying, singing and mask dancing with *hamatsa*-men jumping in through the roof-hole and biting people, and at the end of the show they decided you were a man.

Well, he had served his three days, here on this god-forsaken ridgetop, not eating, not sleeping, and when he showed up in the morning Grandfather would call him a man and give him a gasboat. Not that he especially wanted to go fishing. He wanted to be a mechanic in a big city garage, where you never saw a spruce tree, where you got your hands into the guts of a dozen different cars in a day.

It was damp and cold up here, and very boring. Chuck-Charley reached for the bottle of loganberry wine between his knees. Cheating, maybe; but the rules just said you weren't to eat or sleep. They didn't tell you anything about not having a shot to warm you.

He had cheered himself with a couple of nips earlier in the evening, but this time he really drank. The raw, rough wine kindled a fire in his empty stomach and increased the hunger giddiness that had begun to plague him after the second day.

The fog had rolled in off the sea again. It was playing queer tricks among the hills. Watching the wraiths that twisted and changed, endlessly drifting, you could almost believe Grandfather Koskima's malarkey in spite of having gone to school and been made into a Christian by Father Jerome.

Chuck-Charley shivered. *Nuts to that old-time stuff!* he told himself, and reached again for the bottle.

A fog tongue licked over the summit on which he squatted. Gulping wine, head thrown back, Chuck-Charley stared past the bottle into depthless, eddying gray. The wine hit him suddenly. One minute he was halfway sober, the next, his brain was whirling and he felt warm and incredibly light in all his body, ready to fight or to sing.

A humming beat against his addled brain. The humming deepened, a hum with a cough mixed in it, bearing down upon him from the southeast till it roughened to

22

the clatter of a runaway locomotive in the sky. Chuck-Charley's bottle slithered through his fingers, but he did not hear the crash of glass. The din above him stifled all other sound. He glimpsed through the fog a vast, on-rushing shadow that dragged the wind behind it. He flattened himself as the shadow swept over, its wind pressing like a physical weight upon him.

Face burrowed to the rock, shiver racing shiver along his legs and back, he tried to dredge up a 'Hail Mary.' But between terror and too much wine taken he was all Indian again, and the prayer lost itself in a gobble forced outward by panic flesh that cringed waiting the rip of talons.

Its claws are the lightning, my son. . . . The words were the chief's, Grandfather Koskima's, impressed on the plastic mind and spirit before Father Jerome and the teachers at the white men's school ever got hold of the wilderness boy. *The bird flaps its wings among the mountains and the beat of its wings is the thunder.* . . .

Shadow and wind had passed, but he lay on the bluff a long time, long enough for the echoes of the last loud clap to circle the peaks and mutter away into silence. Then he slid and scrambled four thousand feet down to the valley, and without regard for ripped clothes and lacerated hide, plunged through devil's club jungles toward the river trail.

The village was still asleep when, two hours after day-break, he staggered out of the woods. He hammered at Alex Prince's door. The old cougar hunter came grumbling and yawning in his underwear, his rifle in his fist.

"Chuck-Charley," he said, and grunted his displeasure. "It's a damn good thing de Fadder ain't here!" He took

23

the shaking, hiccuping wreck by the shoulder and steered him into the house. Curiosity sharpened his heavy voice. "What you been doin' to yourself? What happened to you back dere anyhow?"

Chuck-Charley shook his head. He lifted a hand and pressed it across his mouth in a gesture old as his race. The wonder he had heard and seen in the mountains through the loganberry haze must not be revealed. Better if he didn't even let himself think about it. A man who sees the thunderbird is a man apart, chosen to lead his people, and Chuck-Charley had no slightest wish to lead. He wanted only to get out, go free, be a garage mechanic downcoast. Even more shattering to a mind tugged between opposing cultures since birth was the knowledge that something he had long ago lost faith in was after all true: that Grandfather Koskima was right and Father Jerome and the white men dead wrong. The prospect appalled him.

"You got a jug, Alex?" he croaked. "I need a drink. I'm goin' get drunk and stay dat way for a year!"

❦

THEY TOLLED FLIGHT THREE ALL THAT NIGHT, THE RADIO calls crisscrossing monotonously in empty air. The sky was graying for dawn when a tired operator pushed back his headset.

"If they're down," he said to John Brandreth's wide back, "they aren't receiving, that's for sure."

24

"What do you mean, 'if'?" Brandreth asked him. He was a maintenance foreman and had no business in the tower, but there were few doors closed to the large, quiet man. He had stayed out yesterday evening for no other reason than to enjoy Ardagh's pleasure at having the children again, and had hung around all night, waiting for what news might come in. "She's down, all right. Been down for hours."

In his mind, deepening his weariness, was the knowledge of how the thing would unfold. It was a familiar pattern. Already, the line would be hunting up and notifying passengers' relatives. Then the papers would have it, and he could read the yet-unwritten headlines, the same ones he had seen too many times before:

AIRLINER MISSING WITH 40 ON BOARD

Then the long, grinding heartbreak of the search, and the end of it an oil slick in the Pacific, or wreckage on a mountainside—a blasted instrument panel and a logbook whose final entries might throw light on the riddle posed by every air disaster. Or maybe no wreckage, no oil slick, no answer at all.

"If they were in settled country," Brandreth said from the windows, "we'd have it by now." He turned, the frown tugging sparse, sandy eyebrows together. "Vince Ardagh's kids were on board."

"The charter guy? The tough blond? I didn't know he was a family man."

Brandreth grunted. "He is and he isn't," he said. "I believe he went back to his base. I'll wander over that way."

The war, their part of it at least, was long past, but he still thought of Ardagh as his captain. He wondered now, tramping out through the parking area and across the highway toward the straggle of seaplane hangars by the river, how the Captain was going to take it. He had been hit pretty hard and pretty often this last couple of years, his wife stalling out on him and all, and a man reaches a point where he lacks the heart to come up for more. The Captain had taken to keeping his bottle a shade too handy. He'd lost a charter only a few days ago by tying one on at the wrong time, and the word was that Upcoast couldn't stand to lose charters.

John Brandreth was a man of scant bitterness, but he thought of the Captain's wife, his ex-wife, with a contemptuous anger that hardened his mouth. The intuition which briefed him on people and that rarely went wrong had given him a straight steer on Nora. He wouldn't say she had not been in love with the Captain back there at the start—as much in love as she could be with anyone—but that was only one consideration, and perhaps a secondary one. In those days she wasn't anything more than a startlingly pretty kid in a U.S.O. troupe; so far from the top that it wasn't even remotely in sight. But Ardagh was on top, the way a fighter pilot with a good score was in those years, and he was willing to share the spotlight with her.

Hell, more than willing. So eager it hurt to watch him. He'd been a pushover for Nora Stead. A smart girl, but not smart enough. She'd looked for the spotlight to keep on shining; she had never expected the Captain to turn out a sucker for home life, the way it sometimes is with guys who have never known much of that. When Don was five and Janet six months, there'd been a talent contest, a newspaper promotion stunt with a screen test for the prize. With that under her belt, she was set. A year later her name was in lights and she had to cut the Captain loose.

The worst thing she'd done, the unforgivable thing, was to take the children. Not because she loved them—of that Brandreth was cynically convinced. She had grabbed them up just as she would have grabbed a couple of pretty dolls, the kind some women keep on their dresser, and that had bust the Captain as nothing else could have bust him.

They'd cast her in young mother roles, her first two pictures. Maybe the smart girl had simply taken the kids for window dressing.

Brandreth cut north toward the dilapidated Upcoast Airways hangar, the last of the string on the river bank. The splutter of a warming engine reached him as he came in sight of the ramp. He looked down-slope and saw Ardagh's Viking IV alongside the landing, chunky against the river's tarnished silver.

The big man wasn't supposed to run, but he broke into a labored canter. While he was still beyond shouting range, the yellow seaplane taxied out to the stream. He halted, panting, and watched her nose round into the breeze. Her engine roared. Ardagh kicked her aloft in a short run. The Viking climbed into the sunrise, banked, and straightened away on a northeasterly course.

Brandreth jogged on down. He let himself into the hangar, and at the top of the ramp that slanted to the river, almost bumped into a black-haired girl in a blue coat. She stood by the launching winch with both hands pushed into her pockets, looking northeast on the path the seaplane had taken.

His "Morning" startled her, and she whirled with a soft gasp.

"Friend of his?" Brandreth asked her.

"I'm a reporter. *Telegram*."

"One of those, eh?" He didn't much care for reporters. "Well, we all got to make a living somehow." He watched the black speck which was the Viking dwindle from sight, then asked her, "What kind of shape was he in?"

"I don't know." The girl answered him without turning. "He—he didn't say much."

"I mean was he sober or corned?"

"Sober. I got him to take one drink, which he needed badly. That was several hours ago." She turned then, color in her cheeks, and said to him rather sharply, "Who are you? Why are you asking about him?"

"Name's Brandreth. Used to be his crew chief. I suppose you're going back to your paper and write a piece about this?"

The girl said, "We all have to make a living somehow, Mr. Brandreth," and he chuckled, nodding his large and tousled head.

"I walked into that one. Look, I'm heading for town. Can I give you a lift?"

"Thanks." She studied him a minute, gray eyes thoughtful. "What chance is there of finding them?"

"Alive?"

She nodded, and he said, "Not too much. A seaplane,

28

you can put it down in a lot of places. I know a guy put one down in a wheat field when he couldn't find water. But one of the big fellows gets caught off base and he's inclined to be up the creek." He had been rolling a cigarette with pipe tobacco from a worn pouch. He struck a match on his thumbnail and lit up very deliberately. "There's a spur of the coast range runs down to the valley out Saghallie way. My guess is she shot for the emergency field at Saghallie, missed, and is in there." He squinted past her at an outbound fishboat. "But she could be anywhere within three hundred miles. That covers a lot of country."

"They could be alive, though."

"They could be. It's possible."

Brandreth turned away from the ramp and they left the hangar. They walked slowly through wet grass, the sun high enough now to warm their shoulders. Jule pursued her question. "You don't think there's any real chance, do you?"

"This for the piece you're writing?"

"No."

"The odds against finding them all alive," Brandreth told her, "are about the same as against landing a winner in the Irish. To bring anyone out alive, that'd be like drawing a starter. A very long chance." He looked at her, a direct and weighing glance, and she felt he was shaping some private judgment. "What's your name?"

"Julia Thorne."

"You his girl friend?"

"No!" She felt her cheeks flushing, and said stiffly, "Mr. Ardagh is on my list of calls. And I'm very sorry for him."

Brandreth's car was an ancient green jalopy. He told her, amiably now, "Kind of hold that door shut, will you? The catch is tricky."

A coupé swung off the highway as they left the parking area. Car and driver were familiar, and so was the press camera amid a litter of flash bulbs on the ledge above the seat. Worry, a different sort of worry, nudged into Jule's mind. The *Herald* had put Rick Hyatt on it—Rick, and likely half a dozen other men. She should have called McDevitt and told him what was happening, even if it meant getting him out of bed. She had never been in on a really big story before, and she felt suddenly lost and unsure of herself. Probably she ought to be running around like mad, talking to airline and Department of Transport officials, getting all the facts.

"Your opposition, huh?" Brandreth had spotted the press camera too. His eyes were squinted between little rolls of fat; he drove fast, both hands low on the wheel. "So the rat race commences."

She tried to come up with a sharp reply, but he kept on talking around his dead cigarette in a calm and thoughtful way.

"I suppose he's certain the kids are on board. They mightn't have been, you know. I remember Nora, his wife, used to claim she was psychic. Maybe she was psychic enough to keep 'em off that flight."

"They were on it," Jule said. "Mr. Ardagh phoned her to make sure."

"And she's coming up here, I suppose?"

"On the next plane. She's dropping everything, naturally."

"Oh, naturally."

Jule glanced at him, startled and a little shocked. But he wasn't kidding her; his flat face was grave, almost sad.

"What do you mean, Mr. Brandreth?"

He kited the sedan around an oil tanker. "I mean," he said, "that all the world's orphans aren't in the orphanages, Miss Thorne."

The man irritated her. She was weary and drained out, and increasingly worried about her reception at the office. "All I know about Nora Stead," she told him, "is that she's a very good actress. But they're her children as well as his, and I think you're forgetting that!"

"The Captain ever tell you about Nora?"

"The who?"

"Ardagh. I got used to calling him Captain in the Air Force. The habit sticks."

"No. He never mentioned her until last night."

"It might be he'll talk about her one day, when he's sufficiently lubricated. A beautiful woman, Nora. He married her the autumn of 1942. The day after we got Stateside in '46, we came up here to make our fortunes."

"You mean you were with him at Upcoast?"

"Yes. For a while. But Nora always felt, kind of, that two was company." He added quietly, "I'd be back there with him now, if he'd let me work without pay."

He was silent after that, occupying himself with the thickening traffic. A block from the *Telegram* Building he pulled in to the curb.

"Here's where I turn off," he said. "You better catch some sleep when you can. You look like you'd been dragged through a mousehole."

The car door, which had tugged against her hand at each corner, now locked itself. Brandreth let her struggle with it for a minute, then reached across her knees to the handle.

"Perversity of the inanimate," he said. "You mind if I give you one piece of advice, Miss Thorne?"

"Go ahead."

"Don't fret too much about the Captain. You might get to liking him, and it wouldn't be good. He never did see Nora the way I saw her."

"I've told you, Mr. Brandreth, I'm sorry for him. Believe me, that's all. I'd help him if I could. When he went up this morning I wasn't even sure he knew where he was going or what he would do."

"No," Brandreth said. "No, it wasn't like that with him." His hand, freckled and scarred, tested the door handle slowly, jiggling and shoving. His eyes were somber in his friendly, ugly face. As if she were really seeing him for the first time, Jule realized that Brandreth was deeply distressed.

"I'll tell you," he said. "There were two things he might have done. One was get drunk and stay drunk. Since he hasn't done that, he will hunt for his children till he finds them. He's hunting them now. Hell, he knew where he was going when he took off. The Captain is sifting the Saghallie Range for them, the spur I told you about, and if he spots that aircraft or any part of it, he will get to it. He'll power stall into a snowfield if it means reaching his kids an hour sooner. Until he finds them he won't know you're alive, or me either. He won't know any of us are alive, except maybe Nora Stead."

32

The door opened, and Brandreth took his hand away. "You want to help him," he said. "So do I. I'll see that his ship stays airworthy and that he don't get himself grounded for busting too many regulations. You can help, you and your paper, by not letting anyone turn this into a publicity stunt. If you have to shovel on the guff, lay it on the kids. Make 'em the most important damn brats in the world."

The traffic swallowed Brandreth's jalopy. Jule looked north toward the dirty brown lozenge of the *Telegram* Building, then crossed the street to a drugstore and called the city desk on the pay phone. Being bawled out by McDevitt was bad enough without having to face him. But the city editor only told her crisply, "Relieve Thorson at Hotel Maquinna, Miss Thorne. Interview Nora Stead when she arrives. Don't write it, phone it in."

She went out, relieved, to catch a street car. Bob Thorson, the *Telegram*'s top general assignment reporter, was lounging on his shoulders in a red leather armchair in the hotel lobby. He greeted her with a languid "Hi, Jule," and got up in sections, a tall and casual man with lazy eyes in a handsome face. "I'm told Nora Stead rates a motorcycle convoy," he said. "There'll be little men tacking down a new red carpet presently."

Jule went down to the hotel cafeteria for coffee, then returned to wait, stiff and nervous, in a lobby chair. It was close to ten o'clock before she heard the descending wail of sirens in the street. A bulky man in light gray topcoat and fedora came in. The woman who clung to his arm moved like a sleepwalker, staring straight ahead of her. She was tall, taller than she seemed in her pictures, and

33

bareheaded, her hair brighter than auburn above the dead white of her oval face. She was as Brandreth had said, beautiful.

Rick Hyatt mooched behind them, dangling his camera. He gave Jule a lift of his hand, and she got up and crossed to the elevators.

"Miss Stead?"

The tall woman did not look at her, but the man in the gray coat half-turned.

"Later," he said. "Miss Stead is pretty badly broken up right now." He smiled easily, his teeth white against his dark tan. "I'm sure you'll understand."

The elevator doors closed.

"Touching," Rick Hyatt murmured. "Chokes you right up, don't it, Jule?"

"It does!" she snapped, longing to wipe the grin off his flat face.

"You know," Hyatt said, "I had to tag Nora for a week once, back when she won that *Herald* talent contest. She's a scene-stealer. Even goofed up as she is now, she's a scene-stealer."

"I don't believe it, Rick." She was truly angry now, her cheeks flaming.

"That's because you've got a kind heart," the photographer said. "A kind heart's a nice thing to have, just so you don't trip over it. I'll tell you something else, Jule. She didn't want to come up here. The way I picked it off the airport grapevine, that trouble-shooter of hers, Connor, he had to practically drag her on board and knock her out with sleeping pills." Hyatt swung his camera gently. He grinned at her still, but his eyes, more yellow

34

than brown, did not smile. "Nora's scared stiff of flying," he said, "but did that stop her from turning her kids over to a stewardess for a night flight in dirty weather?"

Jule couldn't answer him. She stood looking down at her scuffed and muddied pumps, while anger faded out of her. She felt chastened somehow, and ashamed; she had been thinking more about Ardagh and the story than of the children. But she saw them very clearly and suddenly now, through stinging tears.

Eight years old, and two and a half. They'd be dressed for the city. The little girl would probably have a doll. Their bodies would be small, a great deal smaller than the others, and up where they lay there would be no kind birds to heap them a blanket of leaves.

THE YELLOW VIKING LUMBERED ON A NORTHEAST COURSE AT three thousand feet, visibility unlimited beyond the haze of her airscrew. Tagish drowsed in the right-hand seat. He had curled down at once as he always did at the start of a long haul. Ardagh had removed the two rear seats, cutting weight by a few pounds and increasing his freight space. A roll of tarps was his sole cargo except for the bush pilots' standard emergency kit in the tail compartment.

He paid only casual heed to the valley over which the seaplane trailed her cruciform shadow. If Flight Three were down anywhere in that ragged checkerboard of farms and bushlots, she'd have been found and reported many hours past.

North of the valley, the outer guard of coast range peaks reared white heads against the blue. The fog had rolled out to sea and lay in silver banks upon the Inside Passage. Dusk might bring the fog back, but for now the air was polished crystal, so clear that each gully and ridge and distant avalanche scar showed plain on the flanks of the hills.

Saghallie Airfield dropped astern, and the neat white orchard town at the feet of the mountains. Those peaks stood in fine, bold isolation. Ardagh tilted the Viking's nose, holding her on a long climb till the altimeter registered seven thousand. When the timbered foothills were under the floats and Mount Saghallie's mass lifting from the jumble ahead, he prodded Tagish awake. The Doberman uncurled and sat up. He stretched, yawned, and gave Ardagh a look that asked a question. Tagish had flown search before; he knew about the tarps in back, and why they were there.

"Watch," Ardagh ordered him, and the big black-and-tan dog shifted till he could peer down through the right-hand window.

The river-thread wound past the butts of steepening sidehills. Those hills began to lose their mauled, gouged look as the logging roads petered out. Soon the ridges pitched smooth and darkly timbered, marred only by some upthrust of mountain rock.

Flight Three could be anywhere down there. Unless the angle of descent were gradual enough to cut a swathe among the treetops, those woods could gulp a cripple and leave no trace. Ardagh circled once above a clearing, but it was only a natural rift in the woods, a scrap of meadowland opened by the looping of a creek on its way to the river.

He held the Viking at cruising speed. Timberline passed beneath them, a serrated graph whose lows were the fantails of rock slides, the highs dark tongues of alpine growth that licked up from pond-starred meadows. Under them, presently, was only gray rock seamed and channeled, fractured by couloirs, splotched heavily with the residue of last winter's snow. When the Viking droned level with Saghallie's south face, Ardagh tipped his wheel and ruddered left. They slanted down, bumping lightly as a draft caught them. Ardagh reached up to spin the stabilizer crank, his intent gaze missing no detail of terrain visible from the pilot's seat.

He ruddered left again, passed at four hundred feet over a knife-edged ridge thrown out like a flying buttress from the main massif. The Viking, flying two thousand feet below summit level now, winged across a gulf of air, directly toward the northwest slope of the tri-headed opposite peak.

When that peak's shoulder loomed big enough through the windshield, Ardagh opened the throttle and kicked the seaplane hard to the right. The prop-roar assumed a chestier note, hammering against the cliffs and bouncing back to fill the wild arena with its din. They passed close by a vertical face; and from the avalanche cone at its foot, something brighter than mica scale caught the sunlight and threw it back in a heliographic winking.

Drafts tossed them. The Viking jolted crazily on a torrent of choppy air, but Ardagh held her on course. The rock slide came up over the airscrew, and Ardagh called sharply to the Doberman, "Look! Mark it, Tagish!"

Metal, twisted and savagely torn, littered the slabs. At the base of the cone, an engine made a rust-red hillock. A southbound bomber of Alaska Command had flown into the trident peak and scattered her bones here in a December blizzard four years ago. They'd located that one quickly. The search hadn't lasted three full days.

"Got it?" Ardagh asked. "Know what we're looking for?"

Tagish whined, shifting uneasily on the seat. The slide, unvisited since a ground party packed out the bodies, was already half a mile astern. The Viking's shadow fled on across a curve of dazzling snow.

While the pilot settled to a methodical combing of the Saghallie system, his brain continued to work with a cold fury on a problem beside which the finding of a needle in a haystack shrank to a chore for an idle afternoon. The only solid fact in his possession was that Flight Three had come down beyond range of immediate discovery. It was logical to assume that her radio was inoperative, or that her people were in no condition to send out a call. Logic, bolstered by deduction, became more tenuous from that point.

Coastwise-Pacific, like every big line, chose and trained its men very carefully. Because a captain in a smoke-filled cockpit aborted his landing, it did not follow that he had lost his nerve. There had been no further radio signals after Flight Three returned to the fog. Her trouble must have become desperate, then, minutes or even seconds after they lost sight of her.

The why of it didn't matter, not now. That could be left for some later board of inquiry to dig out. Whatever her captain's decisions and reactions, she had missed her target. She was down at sea, or in the Vancouver Island back country, or here in the spur range which had been a graveyard for other lost and desperately wandering land planes before her.

The events of the night were murky, part of a dream that would haunt Ardagh through all his life. He had returned to his office and the dark girl had gone with him. Sometime late in the night she had poured a drink for him, and, his own courage failing, had put through the long distance call to Nora.

She had talked to him, sitting across from him in the dingy office while he waited for dawn. Most of what she had said he couldn't remember. But out of her words, and from some reservoir untapped and unguessed within him, had come the will which would keep him searching to the end of hope and beyond.

"They're alive," Jule Thorne had told him. "You've got to believe they are. You've got to keep on believing it. I've been through this, and I know. If you stop believing it, what good are you to yourself or them?"

He hadn't replied, sitting with head bowed and hands pressed between his knees. She had said quietly, "Believe it, Vince. There's nothing else for you to do."

There was one thing he could have done. She'd watched him while his numbed and muddled brain held the choice in balance. Then, before he himself knew how it must be, she had screwed the cap on the bottle and opened the desk drawer and dropped it in.

Maybe even without Jule there he'd have done the same. But that was a thing he would never know, and she had thrust herself between him and despair, and he was grateful to her.

He dropped down to five hundred feet, closely inspecting a hole in the timber on the slope of an inback ridge. It was only another alpine meadow, sown heavily with boulders of the last glacier age.

. . . . They were little and light, their muscles elastic, bones springy and not yet hardened to brittleness. Last year he'd been able to span Don's ankle easily with finger and thumb. If they survived that end-of-the-world impact, if the tanks didn't blow or blazing high octane spatter them or sawtoothed metal tear them, they might pull through. The ship carried food and blankets. There would be shelter of a sort among the wreckage, there might be someone else alive and able to care for them. And even if all others died, Don would do his best for them both.

An odd, lonely little boy, inclined to moodiness, sometimes so deeply indrawn that if you didn't know his ways you'd think him sullen and hostile. You'd come home and find him sitting with feet tucked under him in an armchair, alone in the living room. You'd ask what he was doing and get a straight, unseeing look while he pulled his mind back from whatever had occupied it.

"Thinking," he'd say; and if you prodded him, "Thinking about trees," or, "Why can't I live under water like a fish does, Daddy?"

Something nutsy like that. Hardly ever the thoughts which too often, you suspected, made the small triangular face so much older than its years.

The only obvious thing about Don was his feeling for his sister. You didn't look for responsibility in a child that age, but his way with Janet astonished even someone as matter-of-fact as Mrs. Urquhart. He dressed Janet and changed her with the experienced nonchalance of a nurse. When the little girl stalled over her dinner, he would go around to her high chair and spoon the food into her, alternately coaxing and commanding till her bowl was clean.

Other children on the street listened to parents' gossip and sensed the white crows in the flock. Don endured their plaguing stolidly until a blubbery boy of ten tipped Janet off her sleigh so that she cut her lip and howled. Don picked her up, brushed the snow from her snowsuit, wiped the blood from her mouth with his handkerchief, then calmly and in a workmanlike manner, opened a three-stitch gash in the older lad's scalp with his snow-shovel.

The boy's father stormed down that night. He hinted of juvenile court and touched not too subtly on children of divorce, at which point Ardagh took the little man by scruff and seat and dumped him over the gate.

When he turned, Don stood ten feet behind, watching him. On the boy's face he surprised a look he had never seen there before—an adoration so open that it jolted and embarrassed him. Neither spoke, but they went in together with Ardagh's hand on his son's shoulder, the feeling between them solid and strong.

41

The children were pariahs after that, but Janet was too young to care and Don accepted the situation without visible concern, hanging one of his guns on Janet and overlooking her shortcomings as a sheriff's deputy. A tough kid—you felt sometimes that the spirit in the slight frame was more man's than boy's.

There were times, though, when life smashed his defenses and you realized with an aching heart how young, how wounded he was.

Last visit, the night before they were due to return south, he had come on Don in the front hall closet, face pressed to his shabby flight jacket. Don hadn't turned, and by the way his shoulders shook, Ardagh knew he was crying.

"We don't want to go back," he had said in a small, broken voice. "Not ever. We want to stay with you."

"You can some day," he had told the boy, speaking loudly and cheerfully in spite of the constriction in his throat. "You get your six feet, kid, then I'll make you my partner." He had swung Don up, awkwardly, and kissed his cheek, tasting the salt of tears. "Your mother wants you too. Don't forget that."

"She doesn't!" He had said it with a hard conviction that shocked Ardagh. "Nora could get along fine without us, Daddy."

"But she's good to you, isn't she? She treats you right?"

"It isn't that."

"Then what is it?"

"She doesn't need us."

"But I do?" Ardagh said gruffly to the bent blond head;

42

and to himself in raw anguish, *You'll never know how much I do.*

"You come in our room when you think I'm asleep. You sit with us at night. Daddy, why can't we stay?"

There it was, the question he couldn't answer. A judge had answered it, and maybe he was right and maybe wrong, but there you had it.

He set Don on the carpet and reached over the ruffled double crown for his trench coat and the boy's station-wagon coat and cap. "There's a western at the Palace," he said. "You think Urk might pass you out?"

They weren't dead. If they were, surely he'd know it. If they died, some part of him must take the blow and die with them. They were alive, and Don was caring for his sister as well as a boy not yet nine years old could. That was the thing he had to believe. Jule Thorne had given it words—if he stopped believing, everything stopped.

Something else the dark girl had said returned to him now: "You're lucky, Vince. You can search for your lost ones. You don't just have to wait."

Several times, as the day wore on, he intercepted messages from other aircraft. Once, climbing out of a hole, he caught the silver flash of a ship going over, fast and high. Someone in the Department of Transport or on Coastwise-Pacific had doped it the same way. The Viking carried fuel for six hours in wing and belly tanks. Ardagh came out of the mountains once to gas up at Saghallie Lake. Dusk was in the valleys when he homed on Mount Saghallie, and the gauge needle was again swinging low. A squadron could miss an aircraft lost in there, but he'd done a pretty fair job of scouting the area, with perfect visibility to help him.

Deep within him, a hunch was firming toward a conviction. Had anyone asked Ardagh then where Flight Three lay, he would have answered without hesitation, "Not in here. She's in the sea, or on Vancouver Island."

But nobody asked him. Instead, sweeping the frequencies, he caught a pilot tolling the base.

"I've got her." The voice was metallic with excitement. "She burned. There's no one alive."

Ardagh listened, holding his breath, while the sweat gathered in his palms and slicked the Viking's wheel. Then the pilot gave the bearing, and he relaxed with a sighing outrush of breath, and a smile that had no humor in it.

"He's tripped over our junk pile in yonder," he said to Tagish. "No news is still good news, Mister."

They landed at lakehead, and while the seaplane was being refuelled, Ardagh telephoned Brandreth.

"Anything break?" he asked.

"Just a phony a while back, Captain."

"I know about that one. Look, call the *Telegram*, will you? Put them wise to it. Better ask for Jule Thorne."

"As you say. Been twelve ships out today. There'll be twenty tomorrow, I'm told. You okay, yourself?"

"Yeah," Ardgah said. "I suppose Nora's in?"

"She is. She's at Hotel Maquinna." Brandreth hesitated, then said in a flat voice, "She called me a while back. Wants you to go down as soon as you pull in, Captain."

Ardagh rang off. Rumbling south, Tagish dozing beside

him, he made a weather check with the port and got a promising forecast. He had feared this diamond clear day would be a weather breeder, but they didn't look for any immediate change. The mike was still in his fist when a seaplane pulled level to port. He saw Coastwise-Pacific's winged horse on the tail fin and was pretty sure he recognized Bill Grady, chief of the line's Panhandle feeder. Grady gave him a wave and a slow roll, and he answered the salute.

Twenty ships, Brandreth had said. Twenty times one man's chances. He turned his head and said to Tagish, "You howl tonight and I'll kick your ribs in. They're alive, mister. We'll find them."

The voice on her telephone, amiable and calm, was one Jule had heard before and recently, but for a moment she was unable to tag it with a name. Then she remembered him, the large, awkward man at the airport, Vince Ardagh's friend.

"Still open to advice, Miss Thorne?"

"Of course."

"You may hear Flight Three's located, if you haven't already got it. It's a false alarm. One of the new boys Coastwise-Pacific fetched in spotted an old wreck on a rock slide. He got steamed up about it."

Jule's heart gave a great leap. "Mr. Brandreth, are you sure?"

"I wouldn't call if I wasn't. The Captain helped find that one. It was him asked me to steer you."

She gave him a hasty thanks. McDevitt was tucking

Thorson's flash lead into a pneumatic tube, ready for the composing room, when she reached the city desk.

"No, Mac!" She had never dared call the gray, prim little man that before. "Hold it—please hold it!"

McDevitt studied her through his rimless glasses while she passed on Brandreth's message. When she had finished, he plucked the copy sheet from the tube, unrolled it, and impaled it on the spike at his elbow.

"Miss Thorne," he said, "it may be that you've saved us the necessity of breakfasting on crow. Or you may have handed our opposition a beat. If that happens to be the case, your head, on a platter, will be delivered to the society editor tomorrow."

His gaze shifted to Thorson. He said mildly, "For the time being, Mr. Thorson, I'm afraid we must consider your report an unconfirmed rumor."

"But, hell, Mac, this guy that tipped me off, he . . ."

McDevitt checked him with an agate-eyed stare. "That's all for the present, Mr. Thorson." He drew his assignment book toward him, crossed out a name and wrote in his tiny, precise hand. He said, "Have you ever eaten haggis? A haggis, in case you've never encountered it, is the stomach of a sheep, fittingly stuffed. The Sons of Scotia are dining tonight. Go share their haggis. You'll find it a salutory experience."

Thorson swallowed. On his handsome face was the look of a scolded and rebellious small boy. He turned from the city desk, and the glance he threw at Jule as he passed her was venomous.

Jule started to follow him out with some vague idea of

46

apologizing, but the city editor's "One moment, Miss Thorne!" stopped her.

She waited, puzzled and apprehensive. A reporter never knew what he might expect from this neat gray tyrant.

"In an occurrence of this sort," McDevitt said, "we observe a rigid protocol. The emotions, the utterances, of the stricken mother take precedence over those of the father, particularly when the mother is as much in the public eye as Nora Stead. In your account of your last night's adventure I detect a warmth, a certain sympathy, which is lacking in your interview with Miss Stead. There you err."

Something stubborn in her, a thing born in the shadowy seaplane hangar, in the late night, refused to accept the newspaperman's dogma.

"You don't agree?"

It was a statement rather than a question. She was on dangerously thin ice. McDevitt, watching her with his careful, slightly feline smile, was capable of locking her in his doghouse and throwing the key away. But she shook her head.

"I don't. I think Nora Stead is strictly background."

"Indeed?" A parson might look so when he had stumbled upon heresy in his flock. "May I ask why?"

"I can't explain it properly. It's an impression I formed when I talked to her at the hotel this afternoon. It's . . . Well . . ." He had her floundering. "I sat close to her. She has lovely auburn hair, but it's brown at the roots. A man wouldn't notice."

"That," McDevitt said, "is beside the point. My opinion of Miss Stead, or yours, doesn't signify."

He was tangling her deeper with every word. Jule said, "I asked for a picture of her with the children. The man with her, the director Atlas-International sent up, told me there were no such pictures available. I found that hard to believe."

"I don't. My wife is one of Miss Stead's more fervent admirers. From her accounts, I gather the lady is now cast exclusively in glamour-*cum*-career roles. Which only goes to prove my point, does it not? Who more tragic than such a woman faced with the loss of her children? It tugs at the heart. As Mr. Thorson would say, 'The suckers will eat it up.' "

"I thought our job was to give people the truth."

McDevitt smiled his cat smile again, fingers interlocked, chin on knuckles. "Can you say with conviction the truth isn't what the greatest number chooses to believe?"

"I think in this case it's a man fighting for what he most loves." She spoke heatedly, danger forgotten now, leaning toward McDevitt with both hands pressed to the desk rim. "I think it's the story of a very tough man who will probably kill himself trying to find his children."

The agate eyes blinked twice. McDevitt said wearily, "As a matter of fact, Miss Thorne, we're both wrong. Why should one life, one grief, be rated more important than another? There are thirty-eight persons in that aircraft. All will be sought and mourned. But mass tragedy lacks focus. So we choose a focus. An angle, if you like."

He sighed, rubbing his clean-shaven chin on his knuckles. "You did well last night and today. My intention was to attach you to Miss Stead for the duration of the search. You may have that assignment still, or you may play Boswell to the father. Go where he goes, present him new and shining each day, as long as the search commands public interest. Is that your preference?"

"It is."

"An unwise choice. If I had Pilate's bowl, Miss Thorne, I'd wash my hands of you." He pushed his chair back with a complaining of dry casters. "One suggestion. You're young and impressionable. I'd hazard a guess that you've let yourself become emotionally involved in this affair. Up to a point, excellent! But our trade is based on objectivity. Don't stray too far from that base. Also, do keep an eye on Nora Stead. A common loss has been known to reunite an estranged couple, and our readers would . . . eat that up too."

He smiled, and his small, delicately-boned face was for the moment open and friendly.

"About Miss Stead," he said. "Nora Stead as a person, not a public figure. There your intuition goes astray. She's not insincere. She is, simply, a clever and ambitious woman who lacks any true mother instinct. They occur, Miss Thorne, they occur—but not on the front page of the *Telegram*. Good night."

JANET WOKE FIRST AS SHE ALMOST ALWAYS DID. SHE HAD A rusty little voice like a talking mynah bird's; he tried not to hear it, burrowing deeper, squinching his eyes tight.

"Donnie."

There was something he didn't want to wake up to, like having to go to the dentist or finding it was their last day to stay with Dad. Something unpleasant, which he wasn't yet ready to face.

"Donnie!"

It was no use. He was almost awake now, and sunshine was falling across the blue blankets in a pattern not at all like the ordered play of light through Venetian blinds. He remembered the crash then, that part of the bad dream returning, and in the unguarded moment fear swept him, so that he was chilly for all Janet's damp and restless warmth against him.

"Donnie! Wake up, Donnie! Want my posset."

That was one of Mrs. Urquhart's funny words. A posset was warm milk in the morning before breakfast, and milk and an oatmeal cooky before you were tucked in at night. At Dad's place you always got a posset. At Nora's you sometimes got one, depending on how busy the nurse was, or how she happened to be feeling.

"We can't have a posset this morning, Janet."

"Nurse say?"

"No, it isn't that." Explaining things to her wasn't always easy. "Look, baby. We aren't at Daddy's house. Not yet." She had been too little last Christmas to remember much, but he had been briefing her for the next visit since early spring. "You know what? Pretty soon we'll see Daddy and Urk and Tagish, and have possets and lots of fun. But we have to wait a while."

There was a special ache in his head and a general ache all over, but he didn't think he was hurt to matter. With methodical care, he checked Janet from top to toe. Her arms and legs worked fine, and except for a sore thumb she didn't seem to have any hurt places. She badly needed changing, but that would have to wait.

The thing was coming back to him all the time now, in bits and pieces, like a dream you'd a lot sooner forget. The detective had been very badly hurt, but he had stayed alive for a while. Don remembered the detective telling him to stick with the plane, and with his one good arm, groping across to give him the cigarette lighter and snub-nosed revolver. He remembered Albert too, and thought with a queer little shock of sadness, *I won't hear the rest of the story. I'll never find out what happened to the boy with the funny name.* Lying beside Janet, he puzzled about Albert. Bad men hurt other people, they don't go saving people's lives.

They huddled in a sort of cave, roofed by torn metal, partly blocked at the front end by uprooted seats and a tangle of wreckage. Sometime during the dream—sometime after he first woke up and learned it was a very big bump—he had carried Janet in here and made them a bed with the blankets.

Don sat up, and looked over the barrier into nightmare that had not gone with the night.

His stomach churned. He doubled forward over his knees in a fit of dry retching.

"You got a sore tummy?" Janet asked in anxious sympathy.

Don wiped his eyes on his sleeve. He tried hard to keep the wabble out of his voice. "Yes, a little one. You stay down in the covers, Janet."

51

He looked the other way, toward where the tail should be. There he saw only scattered luggage and broken seats, all empty, and beyond them tree stumps and gray rock with a dance of sunlight upon it. He could get Janet out that way.

Half boosting, half carrying, not giving the little girl any chance to turn around, he got her to the opening. The edges of the hole were jagged; he dragged a seat cushion across the bottom edge and dumped Janet upon it and tipped her out into a mass of Christmas tree tops and boughs. Janet liked that. She bounced up and down on the springy heap, and would have stayed there to play if Don had let her. But he kept her on the move, lifting and lugging where he had to, never permitting her to look back, steering them out from among the snapped and plowed-up trees.

They were clear of that place at last. Rock was under their shoes, a slope so gentle that Janet could walk on it without difficulty. He tugged her along by the hand, heading for the top of that long slope. Up there, the rock lifted in a bald knob. It was much farther from the wreck than he had thought, and when they mounted the knob he was glad to rest. Gray moss grew here, with tiny flowers sprinkled into it. Janet sat down at once and began gathering flowers with her left hand. Her right hand was swollen and she whimpered when he touched it. But she could bend her wrist and wiggle her fingers and thumb, so he decided it couldn't be anything too serious. Nurse had given him a show handkerchief and a blow handkerchief. Don bandaged his sister's hand with the show one, and she returned to picking flowers.

"Don't put them in your mouth," Don told her automatically. He stood above her, feeling more cheerful now and rather important, conscious of the sag the detective's stubby little gun made in his coat pocket.

From here he could see that the plane, most of it, lay in a gully which was only a shallow, sparsely-timbered trough high on the side of a great gray mountain. Beyond the gully the rock climbed in terrace on broken terrace to a diamond-shaped pocket of snow. Something glittered away up there. He squinted against the hard light, and recognized the shining fragment as the plane's tail fin. At the airport, the fin had stood high as a house almost. In the snowfield it looked no bigger than his thumbnail.

Above the snow the rock resumed, tilting steeply, rushing up to a tusk-shaped peak. From that peak, in either direction, the crests of other mountains fretted a cloudless sky.

His feeling of power and importance ebbed as he studied those marching crests. He looked away from them, down the snow patches and down the shattered terraces, vision shortening and contracting till it plunged again into the gully.

What was left of the plane's cabin sat near the upper end, stubs of the broken wing projecting on either side. It looked remarkably neat from this distance, somewhat like a queer, shiny, round-roofed hut, its windows all in a row with their blinds snugly drawn. He found it hard to believe that Albert and the detective and those other people inside wouldn't wake up after a while and come yawning and stretching out to the bright day.

The plane's front end lay farther down the trough. It

was badly smashed. Part of the wing showed off to one side, canted so that its tip stuck above the tops of the little trees. One of the engines, the outer one, was still in place, the four-bladed propeller idle against blue sky that curved to the gully's rim.

Something about the wreck, the way it sprawled like a broken toy among the ruined trees, was so sad that Don knew he would cry if he looked any longer. He turned back to Janet, who was still having fun with the star-shaped flowers. She whisked her hand away from her face, but he saw the telltale petals at the corners of her mouth.

"You behave," he told her sternly, and she pushed at his legs, almost upsetting him, wanting to play. At least she'd forgotten about her posset, and Dad would be along in the seaplane any minute now.

A thread of a creek pitched out of the gully to heavier woods down the mountain. Don traced its course to a pond that winked a friendly green eye at him from deep in a valley. Past the pond the woods looked solid and alive, humping and rolling darkly, like fur on the back of some monstrous beast. Farther still, at the very edge of distance, the forest ended, losing itself in a second, bluer sky.

That blue must be the ocean. Dad's Viking would come from that direction, and Don knew exactly how it would be.

A humming first, distant and drowsy. Then a speck high up but growing larger, larger, till you could make out the shape at last, and see the brave yellow of its paint, and the spraddle-legged thrust of the landing gear with the floats each like an Eskimo boat below.

Dad would fly over them once first to make sure they were all right. The Viking would sweep so low they would be able to see the black letters on the fuselage and the underside of the wing. If it came low enough they might even see Dad in the cockpit with Tagish beside him. Then the yellow plane would glide down to the pond, and they'd watch it land there, and know Dad would be climbing out in a minute, tramping up through the woods to find them and take them away.

The little boy watched the sky for a long time, but the bumblebee humming didn't come, and the blue remained empty.

Janet pushed at his legs again. She was looking up at him solemnly from under the brim of her green bonnet. The marks of last night's tears were on her round face, and the hem of her green coat was torn where it had snagged in the scramble from the gully.

"I want my breakfast," she said in her mynah-bird voice. "I want Anna. I want to go home."

It was still early in the day. Perhaps he oughtn't to be expecting Dad quite so soon.

"I'll see if I can find Anna," Don said, "and some breakfast. Don't you move away from here, Janet, not even a little bit." His sister's lower lip pushed out and he told her hastily, "I won't be long. You pick some nice flowers for us to take to Urk."

Don looked back once from the edge of the gully. Janet seemed no bigger than a rabbit up there. He waved to her, as much for his own reassurance as for hers, and

Janet flapped her hand at him and went back to picking flowers.

The little room from which the stewardess had brought their dinners was right next to the flight deck, so he was able to give the plane's mid-section a wide berth. He did not look up to the flight deck either, but kept his gaze doggedly on the ground while he poked among the litter. The smell of spilled gasoline was so powerful that it cut at his breathing. Everything was soaked with fuel, and where the creek water showed through the tangle of broken trees, its surface carried a rainbow scum of oil.

Another fragment of the night's bad dream slipped into place. The detective had cigarettes along with the other things in his pockets, and he had asked the detective should he light him one, remembering that Dad always smoked when he was worried. But the detective had told him *"No!"* in a whisper that drove at him like a shout.

Trying to breathe lightly, head beginning to ache again from the gas fumes, Don understood why the detective hadn't wanted him to click the cigarette lighter.

Almost at once, he spotted a thermos jug off by itself at the base of an undamaged tree as if someone had set it carefully there out of harm's way. Liquid slopped inside when he shook it. He hoped it would be milk or soup, but decided it was most likely coffee.

More grubbing yielded him a wonderful find, a cardboard carton of sandwiches. He set it beside the jug; and not a yard away saw another, larger thermos, a fat green pot of a thermos, half-buried in evergreen trash. It was dented on one side as if a giant had used it for a football.

Pleased with himself, feeling almost happy again, Don

tucked the box under his arm, and with a jug in each hand, started to pick his way out of the gully. It was too bad about Anna, but Janet would just have to get along without her Teddy. Nothing on earth could make him go back into the shiny house with its tight-drawn blinds.

He fell twice before he gained open rock, squashing the sandwich box badly. Panting at the foot of the slope, he glanced along it toward the knob. His heart leaped up and choked him. Janet wasn't there.

He set the jugs down, dropped the box from under his arm, and began to run. It was like racing in a dream. His feet pounded and his lungs labored, but the knob seemed to keep its distance. Her head would bob up any second now, he told himself. When next he looked, the rabbit-figure would be there, busy among the flowers.

The grade stiffened. He scrambled up the hump, topped it, and at once located Janet. She was down on the other side, teetering determinedly toward where the rock dipped in a steep, smooth curve to empty air.

Don opened his mouth to shout at her, but checked himself in time. He worked down toward her, placing his feet with utmost care and quiet. When he was just short of grabbing distance, Janet heard or sensed him behind her. She took a quick, tottering step, and Don lunged as her arms flew up. He got Janet by the tail of her coat and yanked her back. She landed hard on her seat, a foot from the drop-off.

Don hauled her, kicking and howling, to the safe side of the knob. His legs were weak, his relief so great that he couldn't bring himself to slap Janet as she deserved

His involuntary glimpse over the edge had shown him a vertical pitch into treetops.

He discovered he wasn't really mad at Janet anyway, but at the mountain. It was as if the mountain had reached for Janet, treacherously, while his back was turned. He had believed this a safe place, and it wasn't safe. Laboring up from the gully, he had not thought beyond the immediate need of finding his sister. Now, sitting with his arms around her while her howls diminished to snuffles, he realized that his concern had not been for her alone.

There was a fear in this place that lurked and waited. As long as they were together, he could hold it off. If he were alone it would show its face and overwhelm him.

He said to Janet kindly, "You were a naughty little girl. But you be good the rest of the time and I won't tell Daddy."

He was surprised to note that the sun stood directly overhead. The seaplane wouldn't be long now. Surely not long.

Don took Janet with him when he went down for the thermos jugs and sandwiches. As he had suspected, the littler jug held coffee. The top of the other was jammed, and it took hard pounding with the butt of the detective's revolver to loosen it so it would unscrew. He worried the cork out, and the jug was full to the neck with milk.

The lining was broken. Don had to pour carefully into the thermos tops, fishing out the smaller pieces that slipped through. The sun warmed them where they perched side by side on the bald rock. The breeze was warm, too, eddying around and past them in a steady flow. They had two cups of milk each, and three gasoline-tasting sandwiches. "Picnic," Janet called it, and would have eaten more; but Don closed the box and corked the jug in spite of her pouting. Dad might be a while longer than he had at first supposed. He mightn't even be along till evening, if he had engine trouble, say, or a hard time finding the plane.

"We may have to eat dinner here," he explained. Janet needed changing in the worst way, and he wrinkled his nose at her. Their bag could be in the wreck or above in the snow by the tail fin, or anywhere between. Without it, cleaning Janet up was going to be a problem.

She was tired and ready for her nap, but he wasn't going to leave her alone again, even for a minute. He got her on her feet and, walking slowly, led her down to the gully's edge and along it to a boulder patch below, where the creek went chuckling down toward the heavier timber. Although Janet wore training pants in the daytime she was still enough of a baby to need a diaper at night. He washed the diaper first, then Janet with the diaper, then the diaper again. She thought it was fun, and made it hard for him with her squirming and giggling. When he had spread the cotton square to dry, he made a nest of his station-wagon coat in a deep niche between two boulders and put Janet in for her nap. Her thumb sought her mouth immediately; she was asleep before he had buttoned the coat around her.

This was a good place, protected from the wind and full of sunshine. He wished now he had brought the jug and the sandwich box. After Janet's nap they'd go back and fetch them. He settled himself cross-legged in the mouth of the niche, and with nothing else that needed doing now, tilted his face to the sky again.

He watched for the yellow Viking till his neck grew stiff. He was wiggling his shoulders and rubbing his nape, when he saw the bear.

It must have come out of the woods below while his attention was fixed on the sky. It was a black bear such as he had seen many times in the zoo, not an awfully big one, and it walked on all fours with a comical, swaying roll just the way zoo bears did. While he studied it, two more bears emerged from the timber tongue. These new bears were a great deal smaller, only their backs showing above the brush that grew thick along the lower creek. The pair moved upstream till they were close behind the larger animal. All three stood with heads lifted, squinting toward the gully.

They were down the mountainside about the length of a long city block. Don watched them interestedly. He loved bears, and although it was queer to see them like this, no cage around them, he was not at all frightened. A mother with her cubs. He hoped they would stick around until Janet woke.

They didn't, though. They must have seen or smelled him and circled wide, because when next he spotted them, they were higher up the mountain, just disappearing around a rock shoulder. He was disappointed. But maybe they'd come back after a while. If Janet saw real live Teddies it might help her forget about losing Anna.

Janet had a good nap. When she woke, Don pinned her into the dry diaper, keeping his thumb under the safety-pin points so that if anyone got jabbed it would be he. Then they returned to the slope for the milk and the gasoline-flavored sandwiches. The milk was hot from being left in the sun. He poured them a thermos top each, and gave Janet three sandwiches. He had gobbled his own three and was debating whether to have another, when he noticed that Janet had stopped chewing.

She said, "What that little fella do, Donnie?"

Janet was looking down into the gully, her face bright with interest. The bears, all three of them, were in the gully, rooting among the debris. Seen from this angle they had a piggish look—one large pig and two smaller ones, rooting and digging.

"I don't know," Don said. There was probably a lot more food scattered around, if he had taken the time to find it. "Hunting for their supper, maybe." He watched the bears with a vague uneasiness; and after a while he stoppered the thermos and put the lid back on the sandwich box.

The day had been endless in its passing, but now, with the sun a red ball low on the distant ocean line, it seemed to have gone at a stride. It was time to start watching for the Viking again.

Don watched, and got Janet to watch too, when she could tear her attention from the bears. He watched till long after the sun had rolled into the water, but still the plane didn't arrive. It occurred to him that he had guessed wrong—that Dad meant to come in from the other direction, over the peaks. He turned, and the peaks were a colder, darker gray, the snow diamond below the high tusk blue-white now, the tail fin black upon it and no longer shining.

Dad wasn't going to come for them today. Don realized it with a dreadful sinking of his heart. *In the morning,* the little boy told himself. *In the morning, for sure.*

The knowledge that he must return to the wreck didn't come to him suddenly. Rather it crept upon him with the mountain cold. He did not want to go back, and he fought the need with all the arguments he could muster. But already Janet was shivering in her light coat, and there were blankets in the smashed cabin. They had to have some of those blankets.

He gave his sister the sandwich box to carry. Toting the jugs, he shepherded her ahead of him down the slope and along the edge of the shallow depression to the jumble of boulders where they had spent the afternoon. Leaving Janet alone was something he hadn't meant to do again, but there was a lot less chance of her getting into trouble here. He made her snug in the cleft between the two in-slanting boulders with a sandwich to occupy her, and headed up the shallow creek toward the wreck.

The bears hadn't gone away. He skirted them, keeping well to the left side; he was sure they saw him, because the nearest cub wuffed and scurried to its mother. The old lady looked at him, head low between her shoulders, but she made no move in his direction. Don worked his way up the gully, his chest tightening, his mouth growing dry, till he stood waist-deep amid the jungle of broken Christmas trees, in the shadow of the dead people's round-roofed house.

If he waited, if he hesitated at all, he wouldn't be able

62

to do it. He worked along the mid-section and clambered in through the hole where the tail had broken off. In a way, he was glad of the blackness that received him. Hurriedly, holding his breath, he groped forward through the debris. He felt the blankets under his hands and clawed them into a bundle. Tripping and stumbling in his haste, he blundered back to the hole.

His pants snagged as he dropped through, but he hardly felt the shin scrape that went with the rip. Outside, he tidied the three blue blankets into a roll he could trail across his shoulder. He decided not to pass the bears this time. It would take longer to return to Janet by the gully edge, but it was an easier route and the light was a lot better up there.

The unwieldy roll caught on a stump. He turned to free it, and saw another bear shuffling into the trough from the other side. It was a big one, a lot bigger than the first. Skinnier, too, looking as if it had been zippered loosely into its shabby black coat.

They eyed each other, neither moving. Don thought of the detective's revolver then, and felt its weight against his leg, and reached for it, slowly. The gun caught in his pocket lining. He tugged harder, and it went off with a slamming explosion that jarred his arm to the shoulder.

He wasn't hurt—he realized that while his ears still rang and the echo of the shot rolled among the peaks. The bear's rump was disappearing over the far rim. A moment later he glimpsed the cubs in panic flight, their mother hard on their heels.

Don cleared the blanket roll and made his way up from the trough. In spite of the gun going off so treacherously, he felt for it a rush of strong affection. The bears had fled at its voice. The gun gave him power and confidence; it was the bears who had run, not he.

Janet hadn't moved from the cleft. She was glad to see him, and dropped the pine cones she was playing with to hug him around his middle. Don hugged her too, and the loneliness and stalking fear which had come close for a moment retreated.

He found two stray sections of fuselage metal nearby, one in the creek where it made a minor waterfall, the other among the rocks. They were light and easy to handle. He roofed the cleft with the largest, jamming it firmly into place and piling loose stones on top. Janet helped with the stones. When the job was done he poured her a posset of milk and gave her a sandwich. There were fourteen sandwiches left.

He put one folded blanket down for a mattress and spread the other two on top. Then he took off Janet's white boots and tucked her in, green coat, bonnet and all.

She was tired—the dark circles under her eyes told him that—but she wouldn't settle down.

"I'm hungry, Donnie," she announced. "I want my real supper. I want Anna."

"Tomorrow," Don told her.

She had to have something to take to bed, so he worked his cap, the one Dad had bought him along with the station-wagon coat last winter, out of his pocket. It was a cap like hunters wore, bright red so you wouldn't get shot by mistake for a deer, with furry ear flaps that buckled on top when you weren't using them. Nora had called it a silly present and wouldn't let him wear it down south, but he loved the cap, and Janet did too.

It contented her now. She put her thumb in her mouth, and before he had said her half a dozen Mother Gooses, she was asleep. He considered her from the elevation of his eight years. Sleeping, she seemed more baby than proper little girl. It was going to keep him busy, looking after Janet till Dad came.

He was hungry again, hungry enough to drink all the milk and empty the sandwich box. He allowed himself one sandwich, then crept in beside Janet. With the blankets over your head it wasn't too hard to pretend you were in Dad's house, with Dad and Mrs. Urquhart in the living room and Tagish stretched out by the fireplace. If Tagish had been here today, the bears wouldn't have hung around the way they did. Drowsy now and warm, he thought about the bears. Out loose, prowling around the wrecked plane, he didn't care for them so much.

It was the noise the bears made that wakened him. It reached him through the mutter of the creek and the song of the homeless wind above their cleft. He didn't know how long he had been asleep, but the bears had come back and two of them were fighting, somewhere up by the wreck. It was a short fight, with a lot of crashing and crackling and bawling. Then the other noises, the feeding noises, resumed.

Don listened, feeling the hair crawl on his scalp. After tonight he didn't want to see bears at all, ever, not even a Teddy bear.

Cautiously, trying not to joggle Janet, he rolled from under the blankets. The other curved sheet of dural lay close outside. He reached for it, seeing rock shadows black in white moonlight and the creek pure silver, and upended it for a door across the mouth of the cleft. It was a shaky door, but better than nothing. Then he worked the gun from his pocket, keeping his finger off the trigger this time, and huddled at Janet's feet with the tail of the top blanket around his shoulders.

He was sitting like that, drowsiness creeping over him again, when a scream tore the night. It came from every-where and nowhere; it was the voice of the unknown, of the dark mountain, of fear itself. He hadn't been afraid of the bears, he just hated them with a bitter and angry contempt. But this voice struck to the roots of his being and quivered there long after the scream had trailed away.

Alone, he might have panicked and bolted. But there was Janet, and he had the gun. Whatever was outside, the gun made him the stronger. Unless, of course, the thing was a kelpy, and if it was a kelpy, he doubted if even bullets would be much use.

"What that is, Donnie?"

He had thought Janet asleep, but her eyes were open, dimly shining from the blanket nest.

The little boy laid his palm over his sister's mouth, gently, because she must not cry. Above all things, Janet must not cry.

"Nothing," he breathed to her, against the thunder of his heart and the echo of that dreadful voice beyond their burrow. "You go to sleep, baby. There's nothing to be scared of."

UPSTAIRS WITH THE VIKING, ARDAGH HAD BEEN A MAN working hard at his trade. Flying low over terrain where any error in judgment would crash him had been a hair-trigger job, one that left scant energy for extraneous worrying. On the ground it was different. Wherever Flight Three lay and whatever the condition of passengers and crew, a number of hours must be lost before the search could resume. They had been down now for a day and most of a night. Food prepared for the trip would be running low. Another night out could finish the badly injured. And until that night was over, he was help-less.

Ardagh hitched on the seaplane's beaching gear, hooked her to the cable and ran her out onto his landing. Work helped; but when he had checked his ship from stem to stern there remained nothing to hold his circling thoughts at bay.

He lit a cigarette and smoked it, standing by the Vi-king in leather jacket and oil-splotched slacks, Tagish patient beside him. For a moment he considered hunting up John Brandreth. But company wouldn't make any difference, and there would be other pilots over at the airport. From past experience he knew too well how their talk would run.

"What about it?" he said to the Doberman, then re-membered that neither he nor Tagish had eaten since dinnertime last night. He wasn't hungry himself, but the dog certainly was, and tomorrow would be a tough day, perhaps the toughest in his life.

"Come on," he said. "We'll go home. We'll get ourselves a meal and a clean-up. Then I guess we'd better look in on Nora." Tagish regarded him gravely, and Ardagh told him, "You watch your manners, eh? She never did like you two cents' worth, mister."

He was nervous about cars, another thing Nora hadn't been able to understand, and he drove tensely, holding his venerable coupé to the slow lane and making his turns with a deliberation that set horns cursing behind him. When he put the car into the garage, his hands, as usual, were damp with sweat. Through the kitchen window he saw Mrs. Urquhart in angular silhouette. The housekeeper didn't like him coming in the back way, so he went around to the front door.

A bulky carton and half a dozen parcels were stacked on the hall table. Ardagh stared at them stupidly, then remembered they held more things for the kids, ordered during his shopping spree yesterday afternoon. Yesterday seemed a long way in the past.

He hung up his jacket, the same jacket Don had once buried a tear-wet face in. Out back, Mrs. Urquhart was giving Tagish hell for tracking mud across her floors. Her tirade was interrupted by the sound of the Doberman's bowl being plunked in his preferred corner by the icebox.

When he entered the kitchen, the housekeeper gave him one shrewd, sharp glance, then resumed her groping and snatching in the oven.

"I've lost a tatie," she informed him. "It's slippit down off the grill. Here—see can ye reach it for me."

He pulled on one of her oven mitts, reached in, and recovered the baked potato.

"You're late," Mrs. Urquhart said. "Yer supper will be dry, I'm thinking. Sit down to it. Tonight I'll permit ye to eat wi'oot washing."

She and Tagish had arrived at the ranch style bungalow on Arbutus Street together, the dour old lady as a practical nurse, the Doberman as a gift for a newborn son. Mrs. Urquhart had stayed on from month to month until she became as much a fixture as lights and plumbing. After the separation, when he was ready to let the house go, she had opposed him with a matter-of-fact, "Dinna' be a fool. Wherever ye go, ye'll need a roof to yer head, and this one's good as any. I'll bide and see to ye."

Mrs. Urquhart bullied him habitually, just as she refused to grant Tagish status as an adult and responsible dog. Ardagh let himself go along with it now, the familiar routine, grateful for her bossing and crotchety nagging.

"Any calls, Urk?"

"Aye, there was calls. Miss Stead for one." She leaned hard on the "Miss," with a lemonish sucking in of her cheeks. "Ye're to phone her immediately ye come in, I'm instructit to tell ye. There was a girl too, one of they newspaper snips, but she left no message. Said she'd try to reach ye later."

Tagish had cleaned his bowl. The housekeeper's outraged protest in his ears, Ardagh set his unfinished plate down for the Doberman. Mrs. Urquhart was a good cook, but her food was tasteless in his mouth tonight.

"Coffee?" he asked her.

"Ye'll get a cup of tea. Ye drink far too much coffee, Mr. Ardagh, as I'm all the time telling ye."

The cup she served him was deadly strong, but it eased his dull fatigue. She watched him, frowning, between sips at her own cup.

"I'd suggest ye shave," she told him. "The lick and promise ye gie'd yerself last night canna' be expectit to last forever, ye know, and Miss Stead's a stickler in suchlike matters."

"Sure, Urk. Did you get me new blades?"

"I did not. We're economizing. I just sharpit up some old ones on the inside of a glass."

Ardagh offered her a cigarette, which the old lady sharply declined. This too was part of their established routine.

She said, "I trust ye willna' let Miss Stead keep ye haverin' there till all hours. Ye need a proper rest."

"I won't. May go out to the airport after, though."

"Oh, aye. And set all the nicht waiting to be off at daybreak? Whereto's the sense o' that? Ye'll no help the bairns by wearing yersel' to a shadow!"

She followed him out to the hall. Ardagh tried not to see the carton and the brown-paper parcels, but Mrs. Urquhart indicated them with a nod.

"Before ye go, I'll ask ye just to tidy those away. They'll be more a treat if we dinna' open them till Donald and Janet arrive."

He looked at her, and the strong face was set, lips drawn tight and bony shoulders pushed back in an odd sort of truculence.

70

"There's no point in faith wi'oot works," she said. "Since ye're no better than a heathen in yer religious convictions, I'll not look to ye for much in the way o' faith. Ye can leave that to me, Mr. Ardagh, while ye get on wi' the works."

He had never kissed the old lady before, but he did now, awkwardly, on her flat cheek. She bundled the children's presents into his arms, and he carried them to the room with the crib and the rock maple bed, and the walls that Brandreth had decorated one Christmas with a fresco of dancing Teddy bears. Even last year when she wasn't quite two, Janet had been nuts about bears. He had bought her a new one yesterday, the biggest and yellowest he could find.

He had changed to clean slacks and shirt but kept his fleece-lined flight jacket, not knowing what the night might hold. The desk clerk looked doubtfully from him to the black-and-tan dog on the braided leash. Miss Stead, the clerk informed Ardagh, was receiving no callers except officials concerned in the search, and accredited members of the press.

"I'm concerned," Ardagh said. The clerk gave him Nora's suite number, grudgingly, and they went on up.

A man answered his knock, a large and athletic-looking man who had not shaved with a blade honed on the inside of a tumbler. He wore tweeds and a beach tan; his smile was at once hearty and commiserating.

"I'm Connor," he said. "Wes Connor, Atlas-International. Right now Nora's dressing. Got a broadcast in half an hour."

71

"Sit," the pilot told Tagish. *I don't like him,* he thought; then, *Hell, I wouldn't have anyway.*

Connor busied himself with ice and bourbon. "A rotten break, Ardagh," he said. "A rotten break. Nora's been reproaching herself constantly that she didn't go along. I've done my best to convince her it wouldn't have changed the picture, except . . . Well, I'm sure you understand." He set the bottle on the tray. "Soda or water?"

"I'm not drinking," Ardagh said. He asked Connor, "Why's she going on the air?"

"To make a direct appeal. Someone must have seen or heard something. It struck us as the best way of bringing in all available clues." His smile flashed again, broad and reassuring. "After all, dammit, Ardagh, a four-engined airliner doesn't disappear without trace!"

"They've been known to," Ardagh said.

"That's your field, of course, and I won't presume to out-expert you." Connor stood by the dummy fireplace, one hand in his sport jacket pocket, glass in his other fist. "Only if you don't mind, let's not emphasize that aspect to Nora. She's stood up well so far. Uncommonly well. I'm proud of her."

The door of the adjoining room opened. She was coming toward him, and she was taller than he had remembered, and more beautiful. He studied her with a quick ache in his throat, thinking, *Red hair suits her. She should have been born a redhead.*

"Vince." The unforgotten voice was quick and kind, warm with the faint huskiness he used to kid her about back when she was Mrs. Vincent Ardagh, housewife, in a ranch style bungalow on Arbutus Street. "My dear. It's so very good to see you." She extended her hands and he took them. They lay slim and warm in his, and her up-turned face was lovely, not a day older. Nora had always been an artist with make-up. Around her eyes, thick-lashed and darkly blue, was no slightest trace of tears. "I've been thinking about you ever since this horrible thing happened, Vince. When I could think of anything except our babies."

She wore black sandals and a plain black woolen suit, without ornament or jewelry. There were no rings on her fingers.

"Aren't you a little premature, Nora?"

He'd meant to say something nice to her, something confident and kind. He didn't know how the thought had formed or the words escaped him.

Her expression did not alter, but over her head he saw Connor's frown and the quick lifting of his glass.

"I'm not in mourning, Vince. I suppose that's what you meant, isn't it? But it didn't strike me as an occasion for show, especially when I'm appealing to the public for all the help they can give us. People are queer about such things."

"You needn't have worried. They won't be seeing you."

"I don't understand." She glanced at Connor, and the director's face was carefully wooden. "On video—"

"Radio," Ardagh told her. "Not video. This is Canada. They still get their television by pipeline from the States."

"Oh." She withdrew her hands. Just for an instant she looked disconcerted. "Wes, I'm surprised you didn't tell me that. I'd not have bothered changing—heaven knows I didn't want to!"

It wasn't going at all well. He hadn't meant to needle her, but every word he'd said so far had come out with a cross-grained twist. He tried again, while Tagish sat on the deep rug watching them from inscrutable eyes, and Connor got on with his highball.

"Newspapers been bothering you much?"

"Yes, a good deal." She sat down on the sofa by the broad windows that looked out over the lighted city to the dark hills beyond. Ardagh lowered himself beside her. He was about to offer her a cigarette when he remembered she didn't like Canadian brands.

"One doesn't wish to minimize their help," Nora said, "but the reporters do wear one down. I've had Wes take my calls since afternoon. A girl, a sob sister I'd allowed an interview earlier, phoned to tell me they'd been located. It wasn't so, of course, and it seemed unnecessarily cruel."

"Yeah. There'll be a lot of phony leads. Always are." He trickled smoke, staring down at the shadow pattern on the rug. "Lights in the sky, ships going over with lame engines, the whole caboodle." Jule Thorne had said something about an interview. He supposed it was she who had called, and was angry with her and sorry for Nora, being shaken up that way. "I think, myself, we'll find 'em on Vancouver Island. Just a hunch."

He had forgotten about Connor. The big man had transferred from his country squire stance by the fireplace to a chair across the room, where he sat with legs outthrust, peering into his glass.

"As for the rumors," Connor said now, "they've started already. I'm acting as liaison with the press. The job was more or less wished on me, I suppose because I've had public relations experience. I'll be on top of each new development, and I'll certainly do all I can to screen out the phonies."

He got up, and it was a motion of dismissal. "Keep in touch with us, won't you, Ardagh."

Nora said, "Are you sure about that drink? You look as if you could use one, darling."

Knuckles rattled on the door. Connor sighed. He called, "Not locked," and a press camera pushed into the room with a heavy-set photographer behind it. Ardagh recognized him as Rick Hyatt, one of the *Herald*'s senior hands. The reporter who stepped in after him was very young and patently nervous.

"Only a minute or two, boys, I'm afraid," Connor told them. "Miss Stead goes on the air at nine-forty-five. I wish to God we could tell you we had something new and hopeful."

The reporter fumbled a sheaf of copy paper out of his pocket. He said to Connor, "Mr. Ardagh?" and the photographer growled at him sidelong, "Not him. The other's Ardagh. Her ex, you jerk."

"I'm sorry!" The kid dropped his pencil and squatted to recover it. Rick Hyatt said easily, "We'd like a picture of you two together, Miss Stead. Something sort of chummy. Old differences forgotten in an emergency, you get it?"

Connor had poured drinks. His smile was amiable as he fetched them over, but he was shaking his head.

"It's a nice thought, gentlemen, but this isn't a reunion. More in the nature of a council of war, you might say.

Why don't you come over to the station and catch Miss Stead making her appeal? It'd be much more dramatic than this."

"I'll bet it would," Hyatt said. "But that ain't what my editor ordered."

The reporter had found his pencil. He said, "One thing we didn't get, Mrs. . . uh, I mean Miss Stead. About your little boy and girl. Could you tell us how they were dressed when they took off?"

"Why, I'm not entirely certain." Nora's voice had gone quite blank; Connor's face slipped its heartiness for an instant. "We could check on that, couldn't we, Wes?"

Connor answered smoothly, "Of course. I'll put in a call immediately. A good point, son."

Hyatt disposed of his drink between opening his equipment case and fitting a flash bulb to his camera. He said with a certain casual impudence, "I guess those young ones got so many outfits you just can't keep track of 'em. That it, Miss Stead?"

"Not exactly." She had recovered her poise after that split-second hesitation, and spoke to the newspapermen eagerly, leaning forward as if to impart a confidence. "You see, I said my good-byes very early in the morning, before my children were dressed. I had to rush off without out breakfast—a busy day on the most important scene in my new picture. It was their nurse who put them on the plane."

"Uh-huh. Are you still sure you couldn't dig us up a picture of yourself with the kids?"

"Out of the question," Connor said briskly. He looked

at his wrist watch. "Time's up, boys, I'm sorry to say. Keep in touch with us."

Ardagh climbed to his feet. He noted with grim satisfaction that his jacket had left a smear on the pale green tapestry of the sofa. "Miss Stead," he said to Hyatt, "is a very busy woman. She wouldn't have time to pose with her children." It was uncalled for and he knew he would regret it, but the words burned their way out.

The photographer's yellow-eyed gaze was sardonic. "I guess you wouldn't have a picture of them, a snapshot maybe, kicking around?"

"For you, no."

Ardagh followed them to the door. Nora came after him. Even with his back turned he could sense her nearness. She had changed her perfume since she went south. This stuff was lighter, and certainly a great deal more expensive than anything he'd ever bought her. She laid a hand on his sleeve, checking him in the doorway.

"You hate me, don't you, Vince?" Her voice was soft. "But must you be ugly to me at a time like this?"

"Sometimes I wish I did hate you," Ardagh told her. He looked down into her face with an angry and hurtful hunger. In the corridor a flash bulb popped, blinding them with its white flare.

Behind them, Connor surged from his chair. "That's dandy," he said, loudly and bitterly. "Just dandy!" He strode to the table that held the highball setup and started to fix himself another drink.

Ardagh caught up with Rick Hyatt and the reporter as they were about to step into a down elevator.

"Next car," he told the operator, blocking the photographer from the doors, and the girl took it away with a startled "Yessir!"

"Okay," he said to Hyatt. "Let's have it."

"Have what?"

"The plate."

"Like hell!"

"Do I have to bend that rig over your skull?"

The reporter looked more scared than mad, but he said to Hyatt in a climbing voice, "Don't give it to him, Rick! He's got no right—"

"You be the hero," the photographer told him. "Mr. Ardagh has a reputation. They say he's a tough cooky." Leisurely he bent and fumbled. When he straightened, a film pack lay in his palm.

"You wanted it," he said. "You've got it. I can't say I blame you much."

"What's that crack mean?"

"Nothing. Except that when one of my kids goes a block to the store my wife knows what he's wearing, right down to whether his underpants is fresh on or tattle-tale gray. It comes natural to a mother. But maybe it's different with the glamour-pusses, huh?"

Ardagh dropped the Doberman's leash. The photographer hoisted his camera and ducked, but not quickly enough. The hook grazed his flash gun and caught him on the side of the jaw. He dropped, rolling till he cannoned against the ash stand by the elevator doors. The stand toppled and rolled with him, cascading sand on his pant-legs.

He got up, the Graflex still in his fist. His other hand

78

rubbed his jaw. A grin twisted his mouth, but his goat eyes were sad.

"I'm sorry for your kids Ardagh," he said. "I truly am. I hate to think of a couple of poor little innocent punks taking the deep six or busted up on a mountain. But when we get the word I won't be sorry for her in there, and not very much for you." The elevator stopped on its return trip and he said to the reporter, "Come on, dopey. A fat lot of help you were!"

Tagish had moved forward on stiffened legs, an ominous rumble in his throat. Ardagh stooped for the leash. "Keep your shirt on," he said to the Doberman. "This isn't your brawl."

He felt much farther from the children than he had during the day, up in the clean air, scouring the Saghallies. The picture didn't matter, the photographer was doing his job; it had been senseless to clip him. The one he should have clipped was the greaseball back there in the royal suite, the eager beaver who had given him a measured ten minutes of Nora's time, then the brush-off.

He had skinned his knuckles on the camera. He stared down at his hand, and it was trembling, and he knew he had struck not at a man but in fear and frustrated anger at the shadow of death. The kids were into their second night. It might be a night that never did end for Don and Janet.

He said to Tagish, "Where now, mister?" and felt the dog's muzzle cool against his torn hand.

Jule Thorne paid off the taxi outside the Upcoast Airways hangar on the river bank. Light filtered under the warped doors, and Ardagh's big black-and-tan dog paced from the shadows to meet her. With the Doberman padding ahead of her, she went around to the side door, found it open, and stepped in.

They had run the Viking up from the landing. It squatted like an ungainly bird in mid-floor. Its engine cowl was off and John Brandreth, in a dirty white coverall, worked on the engine. Jule heard the clink of his tools and saw the glow from his trouble lamp as he shifted position. He swiveled his large and tousled head, and gave her a grin and a wave of the socket wrench in his fist.

Like Tagish, Brandreth seemed to have accepted her. Out here she felt a lot closer to the search than she had in town—almost a part of it.

"The Captain's asleep," Brandreth told her. "If I was you, Miss Thorne, I'd keep away from him. He don't like anybody tonight, me included."

"Hard day?" The question was banal, but for the moment she could think of nothing else to say to him.

"A hard day and a hard evening. He paid Miss Stead a duty call, and I gather he came away sort of riled."

Brandreth resumed his tinkering. She asked him, "Will Mr. Ardagh go back there tomorrow? To the Saghallies?"

"Nope."

"Why not? I'd have thought that was the best chance."

"Sure, she may be in there. It's still my own belief. But they'll need a traffic cop over the Saghallies tomorrow."

She waited while Brandreth inspected a spark plug critically, then tossed it over his shoulder and brought a new one from his pocket. "The Captain," he told her, "was in and out of the Saghallies all day. If there was anything very obvious showing, I think he'd have found it. I expect tomorrow he'll shift across to Vancouver Island. Fact he'd have lit out for there tonight if I hadn't managed to convince him it wasn't a sound idea."

Brandreth climbed down, wiping his hands on his seat. "That man uses his aircraft damned hard," he said. The look he bent on her was calm and, Jule felt, friendly. "I didn't get to read all that was in the papers about this shemozzle. Did see your piece on Nora, though. It puzzled me."

"Me too," Jule admitted. "It almost didn't get itself written."

"All words and no music," Brandreth said, and left her to digest that while he went to wash up.

Tagish had settled on the concrete beneath the seaplane's nose. He lifted his head from his paws now, and Jule saw Ardagh in the office doorway, yawning and scrubbing with both fists at his eyes. Standing like that with his blond hair shining in the dim light, he made her think for an instant of his son, the solemn-faced, fair-haired child in the snapshot.

The illusion vanished as he dropped his hands. His sleep didn't appear to have rested him. He stepped into the hangar, and she saw that the lines around his mouth were deeper, and that his gray eyes were bloodshot.

"Well?"

The greeting surprised and jolted her. After last night she'd expected he would at least be civil to her.

"Mr. Brandreth tells me you'll fly over Vancouver Island tomorrow," Jule said. "Anything to go on?"

"Mr. Brandreth talks too much. No, I haven't anything to go on. You'd better latch onto a guy called Wes Connor. Mr. Connor has appointed himself liaison man to deal with the press."

"Captain," Brandreth said, "lay off. Miss Thorne ain't a bandit."

On the way out she had thought vaguely of asking Ardagh if he would take her along next day. Now she dropped the half-formed notion. But the pilot surprised her.

"As a matter of fact," he said, "that's what I plan to do. Work Vancouver Island. They might have tried for Pat Bay and overshot, or couldn't set down. That field was socked in too." The frown didn't lift, but Ardagh said gruffly, "I could use an observer. You want the job? Are you free to go along?"

"If you think I could handle it, yes." Here, the newspaper side of her brain whispered, was the break she had hoped for. The other, the woman side, was deeply disturbed. "I'm not trained," she said. "I went up with my husband a few times back East, but . . ."

"That doesn't matter. Just so you've got good eyes and stay awake." He indicated Brandreth with a jerk of his head. "His idea. He believes you might keep a better lookout than most."

She had to find out. She said, "Why, Mr. Brandreth?"

Ardagh's onetime crew chief inspected his hands, then very deliberately resumed wiping them on a wad of waste. "I'll tell you," he said. "It's a dull job, spotting. The dullest job there ever was. A person has to have their heart in it to keep watching all the time, every second.

I think in spite of you being a reporter, Miss Thorne, you've got a feeling for those kids. I think you'd work to find them."

"Of course I would!" She felt toward the big, quiet man a rush of liking. To Ardagh she said, "What time will you want me?"

"Early." He rubbed his eyes with his knuckles again in the weary, nervous gesture. "I'd like to haul out not later than three o'clock. Can you be here at two-thirty?"

"Yes."

"Got slacks? We might have to land. Better dress warm."

"I will."

"Fine. Help yourself to a drink if you want one." He gave her his tough smile, a mere bending of his lips. "The bottle's as we left it."

So he hadn't forgotten that part of their bad night, and he hadn't been drinking. Any man's eyes would look that way after the long peering of a search flight. By this time tomorrow, she thought with a flash of rueful humor, her own eyes would be red and sore.

Ardagh hadn't moved. Brandreth said to him, "That power plant ought to go on the bench, Captain. Take it a little easy, eh?" The pilot nodded, and Brandreth said, "I'll just tap that rye of yours. It's been a long day for a man who grows no younger. I could stand a lift."

He left them, bulky in the soiled coverall, sauntering toward the office.

"I didn't know you were married," Ardagh said.

"I'm not."

He looked a question, and she said, "I lost my husband in the war."

"Children?"

"My little girl died at birth."

It was a long time since she had spoken of them. She wouldn't have now, to anyone except the pilot. They'd both been hurt, she and the hard, fair-haired man with the bleak face, and the sum of his loss might even exceed hers in the end.

"Me and my big feet," Ardagh said. "I'm sorry, Jule."

"You don't need to be."

"Your husband was Air Force, was he?"

"Yes. A Mosquito pilot in the R.C.A.F." A boy in a plywood plane, roaring at treetop height over Germany. She couldn't remember the sound of his voice now, or the look of his face without a picture to help. Eight years can blur even a faithful memory.

"They were tough ships, the Mosquitoes," Ardagh said. "I've been told it took a very good man to fly them."

In his brusque and awkward way, he was offering sympathy. She nodded, rising from the Viking's float.

"Better head in and catch some sleep," Ardagh told her. "I'll be bunking here the night, so I won't be able to pick you up."

"That doesn't matter," Jule said. "Should I bring a lunch?"

"Yeah . . . Yeah, that'd be fine."

As if they were planning a picnic, Jule thought.

Brandreth came out of the office. "Boat putting in," he said to Ardagh. "Looks like a fisherman."

Jule listened. The exhaust thump of a gasboat reached

her in muted cadence. They went out to the ramp and saw a red light and a green, close in, a hull pale in moonglow, tall trolling poles black against the sky.

Ardagh jogged down the ramp to catch the flung line. A man in rubber coat and shapeless felt hat leaned from the pilot house.

"Your name Ardagh? You the fella with the kids on the airplane?"

"That's right."

The fisherman said, "We heard about it on the two o'clock news. Look, I don't know whether this here's any use to you, but last night around ten while we was layin' off Barbary Island, we heard a plane."

They waited, looking up at him from the landing. In the stillness Jule could hear the restless creak and rasp of the fishboat's rubber-tire fenders.

"It sounded low down, and up to the time she passed over us, she was making a hell of a racket. The fog was so thick out there you couldn't see more'n a hundred foot, but my partner claims he spotted her."

Brandreth said in a sharper, quicker voice, "Did you get a fix on her?"

The fisherman bawled down from his house, "Hey, Olaf, that plane you think you saw. How was she headed?" The answer came back promptly, "Nort' by nor'west, near as I could make it."

"That checks with the sound," the man in the pilot house said. "Yep, I'd judge that was about her course."

"Was she on fire?" Brandreth asked; and the skipper hollered, "On fire, Olaf?"

"No," the answer came back. "Not so I could see."

85

The trollerman shifted his elbow on the window ledge. "Well, that's it, mister. Thought we'd better tell you about it. We wish you luck."

He pulled his head in. Ardagh tossed the line, and the troller chugged off upriver.

Brandreth said thoughtfully, "That far, they were shot with luck. Must have got the wing extinguishers to working. . . . What about this, Captain?"

"It's possible," Ardagh said. "I don't know, though. On that bearing she'd miss Pat Bay by a hundred miles or more."

"It wouldn't be hard to do. Not last night, with his radio out and maybe his compass off. I'd say it was a chance."

"That and no more," Ardagh agreed. "We'll give it a play, Brandy."

He sounded entirely casual, but Jule sensed his hard-held eagerness, his fierce and driving impatience with night and the hours lost from the search. That same feeling stirred her; and with it, touching and passing, a thrill of hope. The gasboat skipper hadn't impressed her as a man who would let his imagination run off with him. If what he had told Ardagh was so, they had something solid to go on at last—the search was no longer a blind groping, its success dependent on nothing more substantial than a whim of chance.

Brandreth touched her shoulder. "Come on," he said. "I'll drive you in. You got two hours to sleep."

John Brandreth speculated about the girl beside him— this girl and the Captain—while they clattered toward the city in a wreck whose condition he wouldn't have tolerated in any aircraft given to his keeping. In the Upcoast office, easing his weariness with straight rye, he had listened to them talk. He had been feeling pretty woozy; their voices had come to him disembodied, out of a lost place.

The fat man liked people, with a deep, kind liking tempered by an almost womanish curiosity. After what she'd told the Captain about losing her husband and all, it wasn't hard to understand why the dark girl's face slipped easily into sadness.

She was pretty. Not spectacular, not beautiful like Nora, but the kind who would be a looker still at forty. Nora, now, give her another ten years and her jaw line would be more aggressive, her whole face sharper, the bone pressing closer to the surface. They could do a lot about wrinkles and lines, but they couldn't change a woman's bone structure even in Hollywood.

He said, "The heater works sometimes, Miss Thorne. You cold?"

"No," she said. "No, not at all." He caught the pale gleam of her face as she glanced at him. "We were all set to go overboard on that rumor. Thanks again."

"Think nothing of it," Brandreth said. "It don't help any, crying wolf. That happens a few times, people get so they don't pay much attention. And the interest cools pretty quick in a thing like this, anyhow."

"I know." She was silent a moment, then said, "I'm still a bit puzzled. I mean about why you asked Mr. Ardagh to take me along."

"I told you why. With a good spotter, he don't have

to do anything like as much weaving; he can leave the right-hand side to you and the dog."

A front wheel wandered onto the shoulder and Brandreth coaxed it back. What he had said was true as far as it went. He had known since morning that it was more than just a newspaper story to Jule, that she was deeply and genuinely concerned. She'd keep a faithful watch. For the rest, this girl might be good for a three-cornered guy like the Captain. Later on, when the search was over, he was going to need someone like Jule Thorne. If he didn't have someone like that, he would like as not crack up. He'd start hitting the bottle in earnest or drift off into one or another of the queer, sad paths that waited for a busted flyer.

Secretly, Brandreth hoped they'd never find Flight Three. He knew the answer—it had been obvious to him almost from the start. People don't walk away from one like that. And even given a miracle, the children down in one piece, alive, maybe unharmed, their chances of survival would be very slight.

He said something of that last to Jule Thorne now. "If they do find the ship, it's going to hit him hard. Be a lot better, I think, if she never does turn up."

Stated bluntly, it sounded callous, even heartless. But Jule knew the quiet, ugly man well enough by this time to realize the compassion at the core of his words.

"You're wrong, Brandy." The contraction slipped out naturally and unnoticed. "If it ends that way he'll always be wondering. He'll never be able to leave it alone. There's something, a sort of comfort, in knowing how it happened. How they died, and where, and when."

She spoke with soft conviction. Brandreth said, "You didn't know how it was with your husband?"

"Not for a year. He was listed as missing. When the word finally came through it was a relief. I knew it was over then, and that I couldn't do anything, that there was nothing anyone could do. A wound doesn't begin to heal till the bullet's removed, even if the operation is pretty painful."

"I don't know," Brandreth said. "The Captain's still packing a couple chunks of flak in his hide, and he mended well enough. I'd say it depends on the individual."

"I suppose so." Jule found that her cigarettes were finished. Brandreth told her, "In the glove compartment. Matches too, if you need 'em . . . maybe you'd light one for me. I can't roll one and drive."

He might be around to see it happen, and he might not. But if the Captain married this girl, he'd stand up for him with a lot more confidence than he had that other time. The thing that worried him now was that his friend was still a pushover. There lay the danger. Nora had called today and he'd come running and taken a beating, and, God help him, would return for more at the snap of her fingers.

He said to Jule, "I hope you know what you're signed on for, lady. It's not the safest job in the world, flying search with him. Not this search. You're going to have the hell scared out of you."

She didn't reply, only drew on her cigarette, the spark glowing and dulling, descending slowly as she lowered her hand.

"D'you still want the job?" Brandreth asked her.

89

"Yes. Very much."

"Why?"

Her laugh was forced. "If we find them it's a wonderful story. Even worth playing second fiddle to a dog for."

"I asked you why, Miss Thorne."

"Oh, all right, it's only partly that. More because, as I've told you, I'm sorry for him. I want to help him, and his children."

"Why?"

He had pulled the car to the curb opposite her apartment hotel entrance. His voice was a remorseless beating in her ears.

"Why, Jule?"

The trick door wouldn't open. She fought it, panic rising in her, threatening to engulf her. She had mapped out a life for herself, a good enough life, one that kept her busy and at times even happy. Let other people make the gambles and run the risks and suffer the losses.

Not again. Never again for Julia Thorne.

"Why?"

The door opened suddenly. She ran across the pavement and up the steps, fleeing not from the calm and ruthless voice, but in terror, from herself.

UNDER THE LAMP OF THE MORNING STAR, AN OLD TOM cougar with blunted teeth ghosted home from his hunting. His summer holt lay seven hundred feet above timberline—a cave with a rock shelf before it and all the dark, wild valley spread below. A younger cat would have sought the dark of the cave; but the old tom's joints were stiff and aching, and he disposed himself on his granite stoop to wait for the sun.

He sprawled with slab-sided body at full stretch, one slitted eye gazing out and down from his lookout. Occasionally the yellow eye came full open. At such times the tip of the cougar's long heavy tail twitched gently.

His other eye was blind, skinned over completely with the milky film of cataract. Two of his numerous body scars were fresh; the others, left by bullets and the teeth of hounds, were white cicatrices long healed. Of the new wounds, the most bothersome was a .303 crease laid across the hump of his shoulders by Alex Prince a week ago, when the Indian tracker surprised him in full daylight alongside the trail that led from Seahhost Village to the children's swimming pool upriver. His most recent injuries —three claw stripes on his right shoulder, a blood-matted ruffling of the dun fur above the roots of his tail— he had taken last night in the valley when one of his sons revisited a kill and found his down-at-heels sire mumbling the bones.

Hunger-thin as he was, the old tom weighed one hundred and forty pounds. From tail tip to snout, he measured something over eight feet. His ears were blunt and round; his face was curiously like a mask pulled taut over short, square muzzle and flat skull—the sort of mask a warped mind might devise to frighten children. He was fourteen years old, had ranged far even for his wandering breed, and until his infirmities gathered upon him, had killed on an average three blacktail deer each week.

Alex Prince knew him as "that old one-eye devil," and until their encounter near the swimming hole, had held him in half-amiable contempt.

The cougar's hunting days were almost over. Only such slight fortune as last night's kept him from outright starvation.

He had quitted his ledge with the last of yesterday's sun, dropping to the shale slope below and descending it, stiffly at first, then, as movement eased the arthritic binding of his joints, with a gracile flowing. Hunger had moved with him, growling in his belly, worsening his always-spiteful temper, scouring sun-soaked wits of the day's lethargy. He had survived three mates in the course of his roving, but his mate these last lean years had been hunger.

At dusk, the cougar had glided from spindly timber to the shore of a pond that cupped the snowfield runoff at the three-thousand-foot level. A windfall slanted out to the pond. He paced down it, the cream-colored fur on the inside of his legs showing ghostly at each step. Crouching where the cedar trunk entered the dark water he drank, then raised his muzzle to sift the air currents.

As if to mock his failing powers, his nose remained keen. The scent of deer came to him, wafted on an alpine draft that flowed into and across the hole. With evening the deer would have ventured out to the meadow at the head of the pond, and would be browsing there now.

The cougar turned on the log and dropped to black muck that retained his pawprints, each larger than a man's fist, scalloped where the toes with their retracted claws had pressed. He drifted upwind through the timber on a circling route, more wraith than beast so marvelously quiet was his passage. Although blueberry scrub screened the band from his vision, the deer smell now flooded his nostrils. He drank that promise of good eating for a moment. Then, still stalking against the wind, he flattened and crept out to the meadow. Even at this range, scent rather than sight remained his chief guide.

Thirty feet beyond him, a doe lifted her head. She had time for one snort before the cat was upon her.

His final rubbery bounce plastered him on her shoulders, jaws clamping her neck, forearms hooking for the wrench that would snap her spine. The doe lunged to her knees with a panic bleat, the worn teeth slithered and tore and lost their hold, the cougar catapulted over her head to thud into the meadow.

He was up on the instant, gathering himself to spring again. But the doe was gone and all her band, their white tail linings sailing and soaring like wind-blown fireweed puffs toward the woods on the other side of the hole.

Pursuit was wasted effort, but the cougar raced after them in undulating bounds. Before he reached mid-meadow, the timber extinguished the last tail puff. He propped himself on his forelegs, glowering after the band from his one good eye, his tail swishing to and fro in the wild hay. The impulse was strong on him to vent his feelings in a squall of wrath.

But there were other meadows, other deer bands. Raging, he padded back to the scrub, his hunger multiplied by the taste of blood.

He worked out his anger on a rotten stump, batting it apart with his paws. The stump held a trove of deer mice which the cougar crunched, sitting on his hams amid the punkwood. It was poor, pallid meat and it served only to edge his hunger.

Presently he rose and resumed his spectral drifting through the woods. He moved steadily and with purpose on an uphill slant which an hour after dark fetched him to a second, smaller meadow near valley head. Deer scent came to him, but it was faint and old. He waited in the heart of a hemlock clump while night deepened on the meadow, and was waiting still at the rising of the enormous mountain moon.

The clearing lay in empty silver. This night, no deer had come to the meadow-bordered pond. Unhurriedly, the old tom circled the pond, keeping close enough to the timber so that its shadow covered him. Where grass ran out in brush, he tested the breeze again. It blew cold from the peaks now; and at the tangle of scents it brought him, he came to a full halt. His ears flattened, his tail tip jerked. It was like the smell of the coastal village, yet unlike, for that was hot and live and this was cold. Also, among the manifold strands that assaulted him was no stench of dog.

He mounted a round-topped boulder and crouched there in the hemlock shadow, feeling his scars crawl in the grip of a sullen fear. The moon climbed another inch while the fear struggled against curiosity—that same vast inquisitiveness which in younger years had once led him to circle the ashes of Alex Prince's campfire, so close to the sleeping man that he could have reached a paw to the blanketed form.

Warily then, he moved into the breeze, letting it draw him up from his customary range to the rock and heather and parklike stands of hemlock and yellow cedar that straggled out at timber line.

He emerged at last on a hump above and to the right of a slope unnaturally torn and littered. His one eye took in a picture of trees snapped and splintered and tossed about as if by rockfall or lightning. The moon struck fire from boulders that glinted as no stone should. His dull, sly brain could not begin to interpret the message relayed from his eye, but his nose told him here was the place where the breeze picked up its tangled skein.

The cougar flowed rather than crept toward the ravaged gully. Abruptly, those scents he traced were drowned by a rankly familiar stink. Ahead of him on the course he had chosen he saw a lurching black bulk, then two lesser shapes. His hatred of bears went race-deep. More than once he had defended a kill against these pot-bellied sluggers, but that was long ago, in the years of his savage prime.

He turned now, and retreated to his hillock. If they knew of his presence, the black bears did not challenge him. The cougar lurked for an hour, stirred powerfully by hatred and fear, and the curiosity which now burned even more strongly than his hunger. In the moment before the bears blocked his path, his nose had picked up a new strand so slender it had gone undetected before. The man scent had been cold—but not entirely cold.

His joints began to ache again. He opened his mouth

and squalled once, a baffled and spiteful screech, before he descended to the valley and such scavenge of old kills as those denser woods might yield him.

Now, with the sun rolling up from the ocean, he waited to feel heat of June strike through pelt and flesh to his rheumatic joints. He was close to sleep; but the morning breeze in a random eddy brought the man scent to his nostrils again, and his stub ears flattened, and his mask crinkled in a grin.

❧

SOMETHING HAD HAPPENED OVERNIGHT TO THE MILK IN THE thermos jug. It wouldn't pour, and when Don stirred it with a twig, it didn't swirl as milk should. He withdrew the stick and tilted the jug over the thermos top which he had set on a flat stone between Janet's feet. What came out was clotted and more yellow than white. He tasted it, and guessed at once what had gone wrong. Milk is supposed to be kept in a refrigerator, not left sitting in the sun all day.

"Nice," he lied. Janet watched gravely, sitting with a plump leg on either side of their table stone. She ran the tip of a pink tongue around her lips; the little girl loved her morning posset. Don put the mug into her hands. "It's like cottage cheese, baby. You like cottage cheese, don't you?"

She was in one of her queer, quiet moods. When Janet was like that, you'd think she was one of those backward children who don't even learn to say simple words till they're past three. She'd creep too instead of walking, almost as if she wanted to be what Mrs. Urquhart called a floor baby again. Don had few other playmates. He was with his sister a lot of the time; he knew her better than their nurse did, and a lot better than Nora. These fits usually came after she'd had an upset of some kind, a bad tumble or a spanking or something that made her unhappy.

He didn't think Janet was very happy now. The dark half-circles hadn't gone from under her eyes, and for once she had not wakened before him. Instead she hadn't wanted to wake at all, and had fought him with peevish cries and slappings when he brought her out of the blankets.

It was cause for worry, but not too much so. Dad would be along soon and take her to Mrs. Urquhart. Urk was good with Janet, she'd put her to rights.

"Go on," he urged her, smiling most kindly in spite of the nasty taste. "You drink it up like I'm doing, then we'll have some sandwiches."

Janet put her mouth to the thermos top. She slobbered some of the sour milk down the front of her coat and upset the rest on the ground. Don took his other handkerchief which he had spread on the stone to look like a table cloth and wiped her face and swabbed off her coat. Janet found her voice then.

"Don't want any more picnic, Donnie. I want Anna. Want to go to the bathroom."

There was no use telling her Dad would bring them good milk, or that it wasn't exactly a picnic. She was too little; it would take more than words to stop her whimpering. Bathrooming her was hard too, because she tugged and squirmed, and kept saying she wanted to go to the bathroom at home.

Between that and the sandwich bread being stiff and stale, breakfast went poorly. Janet did eat her sandwiches, though, and he even got her to take a sip of coffee from the smaller thermos. While he gulped his own coffee with puckered face, a rhyme Urk had taught him kept running through his head:

> Needles and pins, needles and pins,
> Both tea and coffee for children are sins!

Normally, making a sin would have been fun. But now, forcing the bitter stuff down, he kept thinking about milk in fat quart bottles in a gleaming icebox. Nurse claimed he was a picky eater, although he never had any trouble eating at Dad's house. This morning he could have emptied a bowl of cereal with bananas and a whole plate of toast, then eaten two eggs or even three.

The way Urk scrambled eggs, they were so light you could almost blow them off your plate. Maybe when they got there she'd scramble some eggs for a treat even if it was past breakfast time. Urk was funny that way. Her voice was cross but behind her glasses her eyes twinkled and snapped with fun. If you teased her long enough and her feet were hurting she might reach out and land you a smack, but usually she'd give you the treat you wanted. Dad almost always gave you what you wanted, and sometimes Urk scolded him for it as if he weren't much bigger than you.

Don realized he had been kneeling in the mouth of the

rock niche for quite a long time. The discovery worried him in an obscure way. Daydreaming like that wasn't going to bring Urk's scrambled eggs any nearer. They were still on the mountain, and he had to keep his wits about him. While he'd been doping, Janet had got into the sandwich box and eaten an extra two. One of them, he suspected by the evidence around her mouth, was chopped egg, which she shouldn't have because of her allergy. He pushed her hand away from the box, hoping she wasn't going to break out in bumps before night.

He didn't want to think about last night—he wished everything to do with the plane and the bears and the gully could be wiped out of his mind the way you draw a chalk eraser across a blackboard. But in spite of himself, while he corked the coffee thermos and tidied the blankets and laced Janet's shoes, he kept remembering.

Most of all, he remembered the screech that had seemed to come from everywhere and nowhere, tearing his courage into shreds. Pondering it now, he decided it must have been a kelpy. Urk had told him the kelpies lived in the water, waiting to pull people under. While the creek was shallow here, lower down where the bears had first come out of the woods there were holes big enough for a kelpy.

The gully was a bad place. After last night he didn't like it much here among the rocks either, although it looked pleasant and friendly enough now in the fitful sunlight. *Stay by the plane*, the detective had whispered to him—but the detective couldn't know all that was going to happen or how long Dad would be getting here. If the detective were with them he'd likely feel the same, and say it would be better to go away.

The decision was slow in the making. It crept upon him while he scrubbed Janet's face with his handkerchief and washed and spread her diaper. By the time the diaper was nearly dry, though, Don knew what they must do.

He said to Janet, talking around the safety pin nipped in his teeth, "We're going for a walk, baby. We'll go to the little lake. Then when Dad comes he won't have to hunt for us. We'll be right there to meet him."

She had insisted on keeping his red hunting cap, and wore it tipped forward on her light brown curls. Her eyes were bright under the cap brim, and she was laughing up at him. Now she'd find her tongue again, and be happier.

The milk thermos was no more good, so he set it on the plane-metal roof of their shelter. The nine sandwiches remaining he wrapped in part of the waxed paper from the box. By a little crowding and squashing, he managed to work the packet into his coat pocket. As he had done last evening in the gully, he made the three blankets into a long roll to be trailed over his shoulder.

Before they were out from among the boulders Janet had tumbled three separate times, and Don knew his traveling arrangement wasn't going to work. He couldn't look after her and the blankets and the coffee jug together. Today wasn't as warm as yesterday, but it didn't really matter about the blankets and coffee. They'd have water to drink—there was the creek and a whole pond-full below —and with Dad on his way in the Viking, they'd be sleeping under other blankets tonight.

The thought cheered him. He let the blanket roll slide off his shoulder and dropped the dented jug, which rolled lopsidedly into the creek.

"Now," he said to Janet, "we'll go down to the lake."

Today he was going to be wary of places that looked safe but weren't. They'd move very slowly and cautiously till they were off these broken slopes and down in the woods that invited them. The best way would be to follow the creek. He tried it for a while, leading Janet by the hand or going ahead of her in the hard places and making her hold on by the belt of his station-wagon coat. Once he tried to piggyback her, but she was too heavy, and it ended in another tumble for them both.

The brush grew thicker as they followed the creek bed. More and more often they ran into wiry tangles that held and fought them as if each bush was maliciously alive. Below the place where the bears had come out, the brush was so matted and thick that Don spent most of his time floundering, and Janet couldn't make headway at all. She was getting tired, too; she kept pestering for a sandwich, and wanting to sit down and play.

"Not now," Don told her firmly. "Not till we get to the lake."

He boosted her clear of the tangle and, panting and staggering, carried her up from the creek bed. The rock lay in a loose jumble on this slope; a few trees grew on the rock slide, but they were puny trees, much like those in the gully now some distance above. The big woods didn't want them. They straggled here forlornly, their scaly trunks gray-black, their boughs bent and twisted in odd shapes, and draped raggedly with trailers of moss.

101

After all this work he had expected the pond where Dad would land the Viking to be a lot closer. But it seemed as far away as ever, winking an eye green when the sun shone upon it, gray when clouds passed over. It was going to take them longer to reach it than he had thought—they might still be on the way when Dad landed. He tried to hurry Janet along, but it only led to more falls, and another bad tear in her green coat.

At first he thought she was only pretending tired so she could stop and play. But after the last tumble she lay on her stomach with the hunting cap pushed forward so that her face was hidden inside it, and wouldn't get up in spite of his coaxing. Don began to be afraid she was really hurt, and when she did roll over and sit up, he petted her and talked extra nicely to her in an excess of relief.

He gave her a sandwich, the last of the peanut butter ones. It was while they were sitting on the loose rocks, among the spindly trees, that he began to think about the kelpy again.

Don glanced over his shoulder, but saw only the rock slabs steeply climbing and the unhappy ghosts of trees. Nothing was watching him, nothing was creeping down on them. The kelpy was asleep in its hole in the creek, and by nighttime when it came out to scream again, they'd be away from the mountain, drinking warm milk and eating oatmeal cookies in Urk's kitchen with Tagish waiting for bites.

It was funny, having your own dog but only seeing him for a little while at a time. You almost forgot what he looked like. Then there he was, bounding to meet you, big and lean, with his ears that looked as if they'd been clipped to points and his grin that might scare other kids but was just his way of telling you how glad he was you'd come home.

The boy drifted smoothly down that stream of pleasant thoughts, while the sun turned the pond in the valley green less often and a chill little wind began to puff among the trees.

They'd have their posset amd Dad might sit at the kitchen table with them and drink a bottle of beer. Then maybe big old Brandy would drop by, and they'd leave Urk to tuck Janet in and go off to a night ball game and eat peanuts and holler themselves hoarse. Not this first night, though. He'd be pretty tired, and he guessed Urk would march him off to bed too, right after their posset.

It was the sense of being watched that roused him to alertness once more. He looked round again, sharply, but the rock slide remained empty. Maybe Janet had seen something. But when he glanced at his sister she was trying to make one shiny bit of rock sit on another, and was completely absorbed in her game.

He'd better look out or he would be scaring himself silly like little kids did, playing something was after them until they believed it and ran squealing for home. Anyway, Dad had told him there weren't any such things as kelpies, and been cross with Urk for putting notions into his head.

He watched Janet in tolerant amusement, the breeze ruffling his blond double crown.

"You do, Donnie," she begged, looking up at him from under the brim of the hunting cap with eyes bright brown as a squirrel's.

He stooped and balanced the small rock on the bigger one, and Janet knocked it off and they laughed together. But when they stopped laughing the loneliness was lonelier, the mountain quiet deeper, and the sense of being watched still bothered him.

"Come on," he told Janet. "The lake isn't very far now."

She wanted to stay and play with her stones, and when Janet was really determined about anything, she was hard to budge. He pointed to a spot at the foot of the rock slide where the trees stood high and the creek curved in a white-flecked tumble from its lair of brush.

"When we get that far, Janet, we'll stop again. You can play, and we'll have our lunch."

That got her up. They resumed their journey down the rock slide. It was a slow and painful journey. Janet was good about it and did her best, but her smooth-soled boots kept slipping and she was so tired now that even in the easy places she stumbled and dragged heavily on his belt.

Just before those taller trees blocked their view, Don took a last look down toward the pond. It was the color of lead now, no sunlight on it at all, and it had come no nearer.

But they didn't have to reach it. Dad would come up looking for them, and if they stayed here by the creek he couldn't miss them. It was too bad the pond was out of sight, though. It had cheered him, and now they wouldn't be able to see the Viking when it landed.

He fooled Janet, giving her only half a mushed-up sandwich, and taught her to lap water like cats do, from a shallow of the creek. He was growing used to that feeling of being watched, and it hardly bothered him at all as he took Janet to the bathroom and tidied her up. It was time for her nap, she was sucking her thumb, rocking where she stood, her eyes solemn upon him but not really seeing him, the way she always looked when she was close to sleep. He found a good place for her between the ridged roots of the first of the big trees, and after transferring the detective's gun to the side pocket of his slacks, put her down with his coat buttoned around her.

Without the coat he chilled quickly. He sat with his back to the trunk of the tree and his arms wrapped round his knees, wishing for the high-up hum of the seaplane, wishing Dad would come, wishing they'd been able to fetch the blue blankets from last night's shelter. He was tired himself, and in spite of meaning to stay awake and listen for the Viking, his eyes kept dropping shut. Finally they stayed closed, and he slid down by Janet between the root arms of the hemlock.

It was the cold that woke him. The breeze was stronger now—it raised goose-bumps under his pants and jersey. Janet was still asleep; although the sun was clouded over, he could tell they had slept a long time. Most of another day had slipped away from them, and still the seaplane hadn't come. The wing of panic, chillier than the breeze, brushed him again. Unless Dad came soon they were going to have to sleep on the mountain another night.

Janet slept a good while longer. When she did wake, it was because of a sneeze. She lay with her cheek on the hemlock needles and sneezed three times, small sneezes like a cat's. At the end she said, "Excuse me," politely in her rusty little voice as she had been taught.

She wanted milk, warm milk, and made a fuss because she couldn't have it. By the time Don had quieted her, he was pretty sure the yellow plane wasn't going to arrive today. He faced the same problem which had all but daunted him yesterday—they needed those blankets. This time, with the cold wind blowing and no rock niche to creep into, they needed the blankets a lot worse. Getting Janet down from above had been hard enough. Taking her back up the rock slide would be impossible.

He would have to leave her alone again.

He put her arms into the station-wagon coat, then took the belt off and made a noose for her ankle with the buckle end. This time he would be longer away, and he had learned yesterday how easily she could get into trouble if he weren't there. The other end of the belt he managed to work under one of the hemlock's smaller roots. He tied it with three knots jammed on top of each other.

Maybe the being-watched feeling had reached Janet too. She didn't want to be left, not even with the coat and his hunting cap to wear; and when he looked back she was still crying, standing by the tree, a penguin child in the bulky coat that hung from her shoulders to her boots.

Leaving her had been bitter hard, and Don cried a little too as he toiled up the slide. But alone he was able to make much better time. Once away from the big trees, he realized that dark wasn't quite as close as he had feared. There was still time for Dad to come; maybe when he returned he'd find him with Janet, or better still, hear him shout, then see him striding up over the rocks with Janet on his shoulder and Tagish coursing ahead.

Between that warming thought, and not feeling watched any more, his spirits lifted.

He was tired, however, and lightheaded from hunger, and Urk's tea-and-coffee jingle kept repeating itself in his brain. Now, as he emerged from the creek tangles to the boulder patch and saw the blanket roll lying where he had dropped it, he hummed the rhyme tunelessly:

> Needles and pins, needles and pins,
> Both tea and coffee for children are sins!

He recovered the battered coffee thermos from the creek. The top was jammed on. It wouldn't yield to his hands, or even to pounding with a stone. He felt the sag of the gun in his pocket and laughed aloud, remembering something seen once in a western with Dad. He brought the gun out, held it in both hands, pointed it at the jug, set himself for the explosion, and hauled back on the trigger.

It worked beautifully. Looking down at the jug while the echoes rolled, he saw the neat hole in the jug's belly and heard coffee trickling out the other side. He heard also, as he had last evening, a crackling and crashing from the gully above. The bears had been there; and again they were afraid and running away.

Don stood hating them, the thermos forgotten. If there was only some way he could make them stop what they were doing, go off and not come back. . . .

He replaced the gun in his side pocket, and heard its barrel clink against the brass cigarette lighter.

The new idea held him entirely still for a moment. Then he laughed again, an odd sort of laugh for a boy of eight, and scrambled to gather the waxed paper from the sandwiches. His idea was so wonderful that it crowded everything else from his mind. He forgot about the seaplane and Dad coming. He even forgot about Janet.

Don carried the sandwich box and most of the waxed paper to the rim of the gully. There he crammed in the paper, weighted the box with a stone as big as his two fists, and snapped the lighter till a flame rewarded him. He shielded the flame from the wind as he had seen men do when they lighted a cigarette, and kindled an ear of paper.

When the box was burning briskly, he kicked it over into the smashed and gasoline-stinking greenery below.

Flames leaped with a crackling roar. The boy drew back step by step from the rim, clutching the lighter tight in one hand and his surplus paper in the other, more than a little appalled now at what he had loosed on the mountain.

The roar deepened, and he whirled and ran. He had gained the shelter of the boulder field when the blast of a booming explosion flattened him. The metal roof of their shelter sailed past him. Something heavy splashed into the creek. He dug his face among the stones, convinced for a dazed moment that he had blown the mountain apart.

But no more explosions came, so he picked himself up, recovered the blanket roll, and set off down the creek. The glare from the gully struck a plum-purple glow from the packed cloud masses overhead. When he broke out of brush to the head of the rock slide and paused panting to glance back, the gully was ablaze from end to end.

Let the bears return if they dared. They would find that ugly trough wiped clean.

Dad wouldn't come tonight, but they'd see the fire a long way off. People would see it even in the city, they'd see it and wonder at it halfway round the world. Dad would see it, and tomorrow he would come.

Don plunged on down the slide, laughing, singing in a cracked, high voice the refrain that flapped around and around in his head:

> Needles and pins, needles and pins,
> Both tea and coffee for children are sins!

NOT UNTIL THE SUN WAS DIRECTLY OVERHEAD HAD THE AIL-ing cougar sought the darkness of his cave in the crumbled terrace. He slept until the first stirrings of hunger roused him, then emerged lazily to the ledge, his aches and pains quiet for the time, his mood more amiable than it had been since his last brush with Alex Prince on the tidal reach of Seahhost River.

He sat for a while like a monstrous housecat, yawning and preening his whiskers. Then clouds obscured the sun, the wind grew colder, and once more his stiffened joints began to nag him. Hunting time was distant still, and it was not his habit to rove the woods by full daylight. But the breeze from the peaks brought something else to bedevil him—the disturbing, curiosity-rousing medley of scents that had lured him up from the meadow pond last night.

He yawned again, stretching mightily, then dropped from his porch to the rubble chute below and began to pick his way at a feline saunter on a course that would traverse the west ridge of the mountain.

Presently he emerged from a draw, one of those numerous sparsely-wooded tongues that jagged up from true timberline, and paused on an outcrop for a leisurely survey. His one eye swept the mountainside. Half a mile off, on the slide near the creek that fed the pond in the upper meadow, he caught a flicker of movement.

The creatures that moved over there were wrongly-shaped and too small for bear or deer. The cat puzzled over them. The brain in the flat skull, the primitive machine that translated the cougar's sensory perceptions at a level far below human intelligence, told him that here was something new in his range. His bump of curiosity was at once immensely titivated.

He resumed his traverse of the blasted slopes in a tawny flowing.

His sense of smell, much keener than his weakened eyesight, gave him a partial answer as his course brought him downwind of the small, upright, moving figures. His tail tip twitched gently. Last night his muzzle had picked this strand from the many; and it was the live human scent more than his respect for the bears which had driven him back to the valley.

For the one-eyed cougar, that scent held the sum of all

the fear that had ever come to him. It meant dogs on his trail, pain and a loud noise bursting upon him in the same instant. His first impulse was to retreat, to leave this troublesome hunting ground for safer country on the reverse side of the peaks. But his curiosity, the powerful inquisitiveness that had coaxed him into Alex Prince's dogless camp that night long ago, contested against his fear.

He let the two figures draw level, then closed his distance, blending marvelously with the duns and sad grays of the mountain, till the scent came to him full and strong and his good eye saw them plain. They were indeed small, not a great deal bigger than the whistlers of the rock slides, and they looked puny and defenseless. But pain still occasionally needled across his shoulders to remind him of his last encounter with their breed, and fear and curiosity remained in equal balance.

He trailed them down the slide, level with them and to the left, moving when they moved, stopping when they stopped. At no time did he attempt to shorten the hundred yards that separated them. Twice the larger of the two looked around, and each time fear tipped the balance, flattening the cougar nearer to the rock, stilling even the twitching of his nervous tail. Had the boy turned and advanced upon him or even shouted then, he would have fled in terror, melting like an illusion among the duns and grays. But the pair continued their slow downward progress, and the cougar paced them discreetly, moving silent and invisible as a ghost might walk by daylight.

They stopped by the bend of the creek where the slide fanned into heavier timber. This time, though, the old tom continued his forward gliding until those darker woods swallowed him. He descended a quarter-mile, crossed the stream on a down log, and made his way back on the opposite side till he could watch them from the timber. He was now directly across the creek from them, and something under fifty yards away.

He settled to study them, feeling more secure now, more at home in the rain forest than he had on the comparatively open slopes above. He watched for several hours; and was watching still, mightily curious, and with a patience that took no account of the passage of time, when the little creatures separated, the smaller remaining, the larger retreating back up the slide.

More than once he had watched a doe leave her fawn in just such a manner, in just such fancied security, while she browsed in an open meadow. Only the fawns had kept silent, while this . . . fawn . . . continued to bleat for a long time.

Presently, though, it stilled its noise. It squatted between the hemlock roots, busy with moss and cones, while the chill wind eddied down from the high country and the daylight faded.

The approach of twilight made the cougar bolder. His curiosity, stimulated but unsatisfied, moved powerfully in him, tipping the balance so far that his fear all but disappeared. He had been lying in a comfortable crouch; he rose now, and glided from the timber to the open gravel bar that bordered the creek.

Janet lifted her head and saw him.

She called, "Donnie?" once, in a questioning voice only slightly tinged with alarm. Then, as the beast advanced no further, she said, "Nice doggy." After a while she tired of watching the cougar, and bent to her pebbles and cones and moss wisps again.

During those minutes while the cat studied her from a distance of thirty feet, the little girl was actually in less danger than she would have been on a traffic-filled street. The cougar had fed the night before. He was a dusk killer, and twilight was still no more than an approaching shadow.

Those were the minor factors that preserved her. There were other, more potent factors.

At one time the prototype of the beast that stood with twitching tail on the bone-white gravel bar had claimed most of the Americas for his range. Now, call him cougar, painter, puma, mountain lion or by any of his lesser names, he had been crowded through a centuries-old war of attrition into a few wilderness strongholds among which these rain forests placed second only to the Mexican Sierra. Fear of man had grooved itself into his make-up until it was perhaps his dominant instinct. That fear was whelped anew with each cougar kit. In the one-eyed cat's case it had been many times renewed in his fourteen years, and even now it did not entirely leave him.

That, coupled with Janet's own utter lack of fear, was the chief factor in her preservation. Had anyone told old Alex Prince, then helping Father Jerome tie up his gasboat at Seahhost Landing, that the cut-down military .303 in his door corner carried a thirty-mile threat, the Indian would have roared with mirth. But in simplest terms, what saved the child in those minutes while she and the cat fronted each other, was Alex Prince and his rifle. That and her own dreadful innocence.

Even before the sky sprouted a fire blossom up beyond the slide, the cougar had wheeled and was slouching toward the hemlock cover. Glare and sullen explosion brought the fear rushing back upon him full strength, and he vanished as mist vanishes into the darkening woods.

Janet gazed after him. She said, parroting her brother as she so often did, "The doggy won't hurt you," and resumed her game between the tree roots.

WITH THE LAST OF THE DUSK, ARDAGH LIFTED HIS SEAPLANE over a timbered height-of-land and homed on a cluster of lights at the head of a winding inlet. Water and air were gray, the line of division more to be guessed than distinguished. He set the Viking down in a power stall, and they taxied between moored gasboats to a dock. Another seaplane, a Beaver with the ringed arrow of Island Charter Flights on its fuselage, rode at the float string below the wharf.

They climbed out, cramped and weary from fifteen hours and seventeen hundred miles of search. A man stood at the edge of the shadowy dock, looking down at them. He said, "You nipped it pretty fine, Captain."

Ardagh straightened from making the Viking fast. He peered up, then said crankily, "What the hell are you

114

doing here? You know you've been told not to fly, Brandy."

"A milk run," John Brandreth said. "It occurred to me you'd need servicing, and I had a leave due. I bummed a ride over with Nora."

"You what?"

Brandreth indicated the Beaver with his thumb. "They chartered that. Her and Connor. Been in five, six hours." He said to Jule, amiably, "Well, how'd it go?"

It was Ardagh who answered. "Nothing stirring. How did she know to come here?"

"Read it in the papers, I suppose. Or heard it on the air."

The girl had called her office by radio-telephone from Zeballos that morning while he was refueling. Ardagh swung to her, frowning, and she said with a frown of her own, "I told them you meant to work out of Quartz Harbor. Was there anything wrong with that?"

He realized he had simply been hunting an outlet for the frustration of a profitless day. He said to Brandreth, "Any news from the mainland?"

"Not much. You'll have company up here soon. They've put Bill Grady in charge of operations. A good move, I'd say. Grady talked to those fishboat boys and he's convinced it was her they spotted."

"It's still a bet. Did you see Grady?"

"It was me passed him the word. Seems another boat heard her too, on the same general course. Grady says day after tomorrow if the weather lifts they'll pattern the whole area between Alberni Canal and Cape Scott. She's quite a stretch, but they've got the aircraft to do it."

"What's wrong with tomorrow's weather?" Ardagh asked him sharply.

"Haven't you been checking?" Brandreth's voice sharpened, too. "There've been gale warnings out since three hours ago. You'll be grounded tomorrow and damned lucky if you can take off Thursday."

"I'll get off tomorrow."

"Sure, and find a Department of Transport inspector waiting to tie a can on your tail when you land. If you land. Better take it easy, Captain."

Take it easy, he said. *Take it easy, for God's sake! The children weren't taking it easy. . . .*

That thought continued to burn in Ardagh's tired brain. They had been down two nights and two days now, in wild country. A third night was beginning for Janet and Don. Somewhere among the peaks or on a rock slide, in the alpine timber or the spruce hills below, their chances were running out.

He glared at Brandreth, and the large ugly man said to him in the tone he would use with a child, "I booked us rooms at the hotel. It's past dinnertime but Mrs. Boyd will fix you something. Hell, now, the weather could fool them. It's happened before."

Ardagh felt the girl's hand on his arm. There was a strength in her that flowed through to him as it had on the first night. Determinedly, he forced his thoughts from channels which he knew were dangerous.

"You'll be hungry," he said to Jule, and stooped for her overnight case.

He called Tagish from his inspection of the Island Charters ship. They mounted the gangplank to the dock.

With the Doberman ahead and Brandreth plodding heavily between them, they trudged down Quartz Harbor's single corduroy street. At its end, the frame hotel stood boxlike against a backdrop of rainbelt spruce.

They passed a general store lighted brilliantly with gasoline lanterns. Beside it a much smaller box, also brightly lit, carried a telephone company shingle.

"Your office called twice," Brandreth said to Jule. "The last time the guy was near crying, the operator told me. Think you ought to let 'em know you're alive?"

She was achingly tired, but Brandreth was right; she should have called McDevitt hours ago. He would be alone in the newsroom now, hunched over his assignment book while the teletypes chattered and purred in their hutch and his tame desk-mouse watched him with beady eyes. The picture woke a queer homesickness in her.

"You're already booked in up yonder," Brandreth told her. "They're a mite crowded with all this extra traffic. Wanted to know if you and Nora would split a room." Casually he added, "Miss Stead won't disturb you. I expect she's going to spend a fair amount of her time asleep."

The radio-telephone operator was a freckled kid with a long Irish face and ginger hair that rose in a stiff brush as he pushed back his headset.

"Got a couple of messages to shove through," he said to Jule. "Then I'll look after your call."

He bent to his mike, leaving Jule to study the wall map of Vancouver Island on the other side of the one-room shack. She saw Nimpkish Lake on the map, and Quatsino Sound's deep bite, and they were more than mere pictur-

117

esque names to her now. Ardagh had put the seaplane over a wilderness of peak and snowfield and forest that numbed the brain and wearied the vision with its untenanted desolation. There had been descents into gloomy valleys, terrifying excursions through passes where the rock seemed almost to brush the Viking's seesawing wing tips.

And they had spotted no wreckage, no oil slicks, no plowed-up timber or smoke signals rising—none of the signs Ardagh had told her to watch for. It had been a tough day for her, one of the hardest she had ever known. For the pilot it must have been much worse. She was sorry now that she had been short with him.

That was a hangover from her ride with Brandreth last night. The casual friendliness of earlier weeks was gone, and she didn't think it would return. But she wasn't in love with him, Brandy was wrong about that. Later, alone in her apartment, she had put her feelings under a merciless scrutiny. He attracted her, a fact she had been well aware of for some time. But it had been only the attraction of one lonely person for another, and since the loss of Flight Three it had been deepened by sympathy and an honest desire to help him. The pilot's friend had made an entirely unwarranted deduction, Jule assured herself again now; and much as she had come to like Brandreth, she felt a certain resentment toward him over it.

The operator's voice startled her. "Ready with your call, miss," he said, and nodded her toward the booth.

McDevitt was cross with her. His silky mildness told her that at once. "I'd begun to worry over you. You've had an entertaining day?"

118

"I'm sorry, Mac. We were up all afternoon and evening. We just landed fifteen minutes ago."

"You wouldn't know, then, that the *Herald* carries a four-column page one picture of your Mr. Ardagh and his former wife. An excellent picture, Miss Thorne. She gazes up at him with her soul in her eyes. His expression is just as it should be—stern but sad. The cutlines and the accompanying story almost reduced me to tears. My distress was increased by the fact that I was forced to view this exhibit with our publisher raising a vulgar view-halloo through the interoffice communicator. As I'm sure you'll recall, he approved your transfer from social with reservations."

Jule waited, and McDevitt, in the same mild voice, cracked his whip.

"We should have had that picture. We should certainly have had Miss Stead's announcement that her place is with her children's father in this hour, and she will fly on the search with him, braving all dangers. . . ." McDevitt's snort blasted in her ear. "You've let me down badly, Miss Thorne."

"I'm sorry," Jule said. McDevitt would have had a rough day too, with the downstairs brass hounding him. Let him work it off on her if he wanted—she was two hundred miles away, safe from the noxious assignments he reserved for reporters out of favor.

"Thorson will join you tomorrow, and a photographer." The city editor was coming off the boil. "Your assignment remains unchanged, but you'll co-operate with Thorson where possible. Another thing: Miss Stead's amanuensis, this Connor fellow, descended on our advertising manager with a paper folded at your interview and demanded we kill it before the next edition. Since it was then dead copy, we obliged him. The man's an obstructionist. Be wary of him."

McDevitt hung up. The ginger-haired operator grinned at Jule as she stepped from the booth. He rubbed an ear.

"Had to listen in for reception," he lied brazenly. "Your boss lays on the leather, no?"

"That was a mild performance," Jule told him, and the operator said, "We'll be open all night, more or less. If you want to work here, you can."

"Thanks. May I leave my typewriter, then?"

"Sure. I'll stash it away so none of the bushrats will figure it's a new-type Geiger." He hesitated, then said, "About this big man from the South, this Connor. I had a run-in with him, kind of. He tells me all newspaper stuff that goes out, he's supposed to censor, and that I'm not to pass anything without his initials."

"Well!" Jule said softly. "Mr. Connor did, did he?"

"That's about how the home office felt. They told me to tell him to go to hell, in a polite sort of way."

"I hope you will."

"I already have." His grin widened. "Say, this Nora Stead, she's quite a something, isn't she?"

"Quite a something," Jule agreed. She set her portable beside the office safe, and went out to the street.

Wes Connor sat on the hotel verandah in the light of an unshaded bulb, slapping at mosquitoes that peeled off in relays from the traffic circle around his head. Connor had acquired high-cut boots and a woolen shirt; he looked a lot less urbane than he had in Nora's suite, and the glance he gave Jule as she mounted the steps was not friendly.

Let him just open his mouth, Jule thought, and challenged him with a cold stare.

But the Atlas-International troubleshooter only hunched his shirt collar higher and reached for the glass on the verandah rail.

She was mad clear through, mad at everyone concerned in the search, and, she realized, maddest of all at Vince Ardagh. He must have known Nora Stead intended to fly with him. And, in decency, the pilot should have told her about that picture.

The settlement at tidehead on Wellington Inlet was one of Ardagh's frequent ports of call. He knew all Quartz Harbor's permanent residents and many of the transients, the prospectors and miners and offshore fishermen who called in for supplies or passed through on their way to the hinterland. Some of the old-timers, like the Boyds who ran the hotel and Doc Bernstein in charge of the Red Cross Outpost Hospital, had been his friends since his earliest charters.

But he didn't want their company, or their sympathy, tonight. He didn't even want Brandreth around, and was glad when Brandy quit fussing with the Viking's engine and took himself off to bed. Then, perversely, when Brandreth was gone and he and Tagish had the float string to themselves, he found that being alone was very much worse.

He topped off his fuel tanks, made a radio weather check that drew his lips into a tight line of dismay, then

121

with the Doberman ambling beside him, strolled back along the dock to town.

No use returning to the hotel. Nora was there, but he doubted if he could trust himself not to hurt her again by saying things he didn't want to say. And if he crossed trails with Nora's interference runner tonight, he thought with a flash of sour humor, it would probably end in mayhem.

He wandered down the street. Outside the radio-telephone office, he heard the clicking of a typewriter. He stopped, and peered through the window. Jule was typing busily at the operator's desk, the raw light shining on her bent head.

All through supper she had been out of sorts, giving him and Brandreth sharp answers when they spoke to her, until finally they let her alone. Ardagh watched her now, liking the dark girl, wondering why he felt better when she was near. Other people, even Nora, had seemed vaguely unreal to him since this thing broke. It was only when he was with Jule that he could come at least partway out of his fog.

Jule had stopped typing. She smoked too much; she was lighting another cigarette from the butt of her last; she looked businesslike, hard almost, the planes of her cheeks flat, her mouth firm. Seen so, Ardagh thought, she was more like a delicately handsome boy than a woman.

She glanced up and saw him. Being discovered staring at her like that worsened his edgy mood. He stepped into the shack.

"Writing a book?"

"I'm about done. Do you want to censor my copy, too?"

"I don't care what you write." The same perversity that had made him seek company after Brandreth left was on him now. "Better cool down before you blow a fuse. What's eating you, anyway?"

"Nothing that matters."

"It mattered enough to burn you, didn't it?"

"At the time, yes." Jule closed her typewriter case with a snap.

"Why don't you go sleep it off?"

She shuffled the pages of her piece together, tapped them briskly on the desk. Then she folded them and slipped them into a Manila envelope. She scribbled on the envelope, the straight, dark hair falling forward so that her face was half-hidden. But Ardagh saw the flush on her cheekbones.

"That's just what I intend to do," Jule said crisply. "Go sleep it off. You'd better get some sleep too."

"Look, if you're sick of the spotting job, if you want to give it up . . ."

"I'm not sick of it! I'd have kept on at it as long as you needed me. But I won't be flying with you tomorrow or Thursday or whenever you do go up again." She licked the envelope, and her gray eyes over its top were smoky with anger. "That honor, I'm told, goes to Miss Stead— which is as it ought to be."

"What in hell are you talking about, Jule?"

"Don't you know she's going to help you? You ought to keep up with the news, Vince. That's why she's here."

"I don't believe it."

"You could ask her."

"I will." He had prodded her, and now it was he who was on the defensive. "Nora's terrified of flying. Always has been. She's . . . Some ways she's a lot like a child herself."

He had never spoken against Nora. He wasn't speaking against her now, just stating a fact. "If you don't want to keep on, okay. But can't you find a better reason than that?"

They were bickering stupidly so, in an exchange aimless and desultory as heat lightning, when the operator loosed an abrupt grunt and leaned forward in his swivel chair. He snatched the pencil from under his headset clamp.

"Yeah," he said. "Yeah, shoot!" He listened a moment, then said eagerly, "Yeah, sure, you bet I'll tell him!"

Ardagh crossed to stand behind him. *Careful,* he warned himself. *It doesn't have to be anything. A star on a ridge top. Some nut loose with a hot idea. . . .*

But his palms had begun to sweat as they had in the tough places today, and he could feel the slow, sick thudding of his heart.

Jule had crossed too. They stood close together, silent, watching the indecipherable scrawl flow from under the operator's pencil.

When he swung round, he was white with excitement.

"For you," he said to the pilot. "A Mr. Grady just got it from a Dominion Fisheries patrol boat upcoast. They were coming in from sixty miles out—they'd been scouting for tuna—and they saw a hell of a glare over the mountains a long way north. By the time they got around to figuring what it might be, it had died down. The nearest they can place it is somewhere between Seahhost and Aragon Inlets."

He glanced at his note. "Time, between eight and eight-thirty. Not a bush fire, it couldn't be; it's not fire weather. The officer who spotted it first said it looked more like an explosion than anything else."

Ardagh still stared down at the note. The operator said, "There's nothing in that country, no loggers, maybe a prospector once in three years. Just mountains and timber."

Jule asked him sharply, "Is that all? Did they see anything else?"

"That's all, except Mr. Grady says to tell Mr. Ardagh he'll be over here tomorrow."

Ardagh thought, *Lightning could do it. Or sun rays through broken glass.* But not that late, unless the wreckage smoldered a long time before catching. And if it were fuel-soaked it wouldn't smolder, it would puff up as soon as combustion point was reached. The day had been cool, with a partial overcast from noon on.

He discarded that plunging surmise. They might have been mistaken. Eyes watching for something they hope to see can play strange tricks. But the fisheries crew hadn't been watching for a lost plane's distress signal. It hadn't occurred to them for a long time what the glare in the northern sky might mean.

He said harshly to the girl, "I think this is it," and Jule said, "Yes. Yes! But oh, Vince . . ."

"If she were going to burn it would have been when they crashed. Not forty-eight hours after. Someone's alive up there. Somebody fired her."

"Vince, Vince!" She had reached for his hands. Her eyes were wet with tears; the face he had thought hard was crumpled and pitiful. "It may not mean what we hope. Don't be too sure."

"I am sure."

"Vince, we've still got to locate it. And even when we do . . ."

She had forced belief upon him when he had been driving straight for a pit of despair, and she was doubting now, weeping openly, the tears running down her face. The pilot stooped and kissed her hard on her mouth, then turned and shouldered out of the office. He had more than stubborn belief to support him now. He had hope—a hope that flared like high octane fuel touched off by a living hand to light the storm clouds above a darkening mountain.

The operator stared round-eyed. His softly uttered "Holy Moses!" broke the quiet Ardagh had left behind him. He said to Jule, "Where's he going? He can't take his ship off now—they'd ground him for a year!"

Her hands still hurt from the pilot's grip, and her lips burned from that rough kiss. She laughed in a brittle way, her cheeks wet, her eyes unseeing. But she did not reply to the operator's question, although she knew the answer well enough.

The kiss meant nothing. Ardagh had turned to her when he was desperately hurt. One touch of hope changed all that. She had no need to follow him in his swift striding to know he was bound back to the hotel at the end of the street, to Nora Stead.

She put her typewriter away, said good night to the

126

radio operator, then went hunting the Island Charter Flights pilot, who would be returning to the mainland if the morning weather let him. By the time she had located him in the beer parlor and arranged for her copy to be delivered to the *Telegram,* it was close to midnight. Tired and depressed, she walked along the planked street to the hotel. He had kissed her, and the kiss meant precisely as much as her own refusal to admit what was happening to her.

The prospect of sharing a room with Nora Stead appealed to her not at all, and the room itself was a cheerless box with scarred, old-fashioned dresser and two brass bedsteads. But she needn't have concerned herself about Nora. The woman was deep asleep. She lay on her back, bright hair spread on the pillow, the light beating full on her face. Lying under that hard light she looked older, harsher, the line of her jaw more prominent, her lips thinner and her brilliant daytime beauty gone.

A little bottle shared the dresser top with the hand basin and ornate jug. Jule picked up the bottle and saw that it was half-filled with white tablets. Sleeping pills. She had put Rick Hyatt's grapevine gossip from her mind, but it returned now, grooving a frown between her eyes. Gingerly she replaced the bottle and turned to the other bed.

Bill Grady, Coastwise-Pacific's Panhandle feeder boss, boomed in on a tail wind three hours after daybreak. While his Fairchild Husky was still dragging the lane between the moored fishboats, three more aircraft roared low over the eastern ridge. Before Grady's exhaust shots stopped racketing around the granite walls of the inlet, an R.C.A.F. Norseman was taxiing down the lane. The other two craft, a second Coastwise-Pacific seaplane and a U.S. Coast Guard amphibian, landed in turn. The chesty drone of propellers continued as more ships broke from the overcast, running like scared cats ahead of the weather.

"A bloody armada," Brandreth said to Ardagh. They had helped Grady tie up, and now stood by the tall black-haired pilot and his passenger, watching new units of the search fleet set down.

"We weren't doing any good on the mainland," Grady said. "This way, when she lifts we'll be all set. That last report could be the payoff, Vince."

"Could be," Ardagh agreed. He had lain awake a long time, then when sleep did come to him, had dropped into a tormented dream in which the children flitted ahead of him down a straight and endless road toward a blurred horizon. He had awakened sweating, and spent the rest of the night chain-smoking by the window.

He was glad there were others to share the burden of the search, but in an abstracted sort of way. Nora was late —two hours late. He'd give her a few minutes longer, then if she didn't show up, take off without her.

Brandreth's elbow nudged him, and he realized Bill Grady was speaking to him again, introducing him to the gray little man in the business suit who had crossed in the Fairchild with him.

"Mr. Langmuir, Vince, Department of Transport. He tells me the Department intends to give us as free a hand as possible."

Grady's tone and words were casual, but his glance conveyed a warning which Ardagh recognized as he returned Langmuir's brisk handshake. He hadn't met this particular D.O.T. man before, and guessed he was the new assistant inspector due out from Ottawa. The Department's power was absolute, its regulations a barbed wire entanglement in which a chance-taking pilot could find himself snagged all too easily.

"When'd you last sleep, Ardagh?" the inspector asked him bluntly.

"I turned out twenty minutes ago," Ardagh said. "From my last weather check, I figured I might manage a look at the Seahhost-Aragon strip before she soups up."

"I'm not too sure of that," Langmuir said. Behind his glasses his sharp blue eyes were troubled. "I'm told there's a special urgency in this for you, and you have my sympathy. But by the look of you, you're about due for a day in. From the last meteorological report, we're not many hours from minimum right now."

"This coast makes its own weather," Ardagh told him. He was pretty sure Langmuir could find the Viking unairworthy without too much trouble. His desperate impatience clawed at him, but he fought to keep his voice as casual as Grady's. "Take around Seahhost for instance. I've seen the weather swap ends up there in an hour."

The inspector said to Grady, "Well, Captain, what's your opinion?"

Grady's answer was prompt and vigorous. "In view of the fisheries patrol report, sir, I think it's a justifiable risk. A few hours saved can make a hell of a difference, if there are survivors. Suppose Ardagh and his observer make a scouting mission of it. In the meantime I'll draw up a flight plan for cross-sectioning by every ship available."

"Very well," Langmuir agreed grudgingly. "Just keep in mind, though, that nobody will be helped if we're forced to split the search. You're to keep in close touch, Ardagh. We'll expect to hear from you at half-hour intervals."

A green light. Ardagh let his breath go out slowly, standing by the Viking on a float string now crowded with air-borne arrivals. He saw Rick Hyatt of the *Herald*, short and heavy-set in a loud-patterned Indian sweater, feeding a fresh bulb into his gun.

A hand touched his arm. He turned and saw a blue trench coat, and thought for an instant with an odd relief, *Nora's backed out.*

But the face under the plastic kerchief wasn't Jule's. They must be hitting it off pretty well, if Jule Thorne had loaned Nora her coat.

"You're late," he said.

"I didn't really think you'd be going, in this weather. I'm afraid I overslept." The newspapermen had edged closer. Hyatt watched with a shadow of a grin, his camera dangling. Nora raised her voice a trifle. "But I'm ready now, Vince, any time."

She spoke confidently, with a determined brightness. Close to Hyatt, a lanky reporter in tweeds was writing on a fold of paper. Ardagh recognized him as Bob Thorson, who had covered airport for the *Telegram* before Jule's time. Wes Connor had come down with Nora, and stood off to the side. He looked like a man with a grouch, or a hangover.

Nora's voice and manner didn't fool him. She was afraid. Fear was around her like an almost visible aura; he wondered if any of the others, people who knew her less well than he, could sense it.

Pity for her softened his voice. "I'm not sure I should take you. Why not just stay here close to the radio, Nora? I'll be checking in often."

"Stay here? When my children may be alive?" Her glance reproached him; Thorson's pencil was moving rapidly, and the *Telegram* photographer who had come over with him was fitting a bulb to his gun. "No, I couldn't do that, especially now there's a chance."

She stepped toward the yellow Viking, shabby among the tethered ships of the fleet, and Ardagh followed her, seeing Connor's frown, blinking as a flash bulb winked in his sore eyes. He handed Nora up to the cockpit, ducked under the seaplane's nose and swung into his own seat. Looking past Nora, he saw the Department inspector turn to Grady and knew he was asking a question. Grady's answer seemed to satisfy him; anyway, he made no move to interfere.

Brandreth worked the Viking out of the line, a Coast Guard chief helping. Ardagh pressed the starter, letting the engine warm while he maneuvered slowly into the clear. As he brought the Viking into the wind he glanced back, searching floats and dock. But if Jule Thorne had come down, he wasn't able to locate her.

Nora's tension communicated itself to him. He had left Tagish at the hotel, knowing how Nora felt about him. Now, revving his engine, readying her for the takeoff, he wished the Doberman were in back. It didn't seem right, flying without him. Nora sat stiffly, both hands gripped hard in her safety belt. She looked sick; her lips moved, but her words were drowned in the roar.

The wind was so strong now, bowling down the inlet, that the seaplane lifted clear in not much more than half her usual run. Ardagh hiked her to five hundred, banked, and came back over the town. He straightened and climbed until they winged close under the dirty gray ceiling. The west coast surf began to unreel in a reef-broken fringe below, endless as the road down which he had struggled in his dream. Something had waited at the horizon for the children. It was that knowledge, the need to overtake them, snatch them back, which had wakened him with the sweat chill on his face.

The tail wind boosted them along. The coast fled under the wing as they scudded north, flying a straight course over the forests and across the tortuous inlets. Frequently now they lost contact and drove blind through swirling vapor. That didn't matter here. What mattered was the weather north, over and around the peaks that rose inland behind tidehead in the Aragon-Seahhost sector.

Rough air over Mechitna Sound gave them a bouncing. Busy with stabilizer crank and jittering rudder bar, Ardagh didn't get around to calling Quartz Harbor till they were across the Sound and boring on toward the northern inlets.

He got Bill Grady in a cacophony of static, but Grady had nothing for him except a worried query about the weather. The inspector would be with him in the radio shack; Ardagh half-expected a recall, but for the time at least, he was safe. Although the weather wasn't promising, it was still a long way from minimum as a bush pilot knew the term.

Occupied with the hard physical job of handling the Viking, he spared neither glance nor thought for Nora. Not till an hour later, with the pewter gleam of Seahhost Inlet visible through tatters of cloud, did Ardagh turn to her.

Nora's head was pressed to the back of the seat. For a moment he thought she was asleep; then he saw her knuckles showing white from the grip of her slim hands on the seat arms. She shouldn't have come. He shouldn't have taken her. The worst of the trip lay all ahead when they swung east from the Pacific at Seahhost and slugged inland toward the eight thousand footers of the Medusa Group.

A night had blown the froth off his hope. Yesterday, even without a red-hot lead to track down, he had felt that the next hole or valley might reveal the wreck of Flight Three, her people around her, smoke signals rising or a distress V trampled in the snow. It came to him now that Jule Thorne being there had made the difference. Something in their impersonal companionship had been right and good for a job like this. Even without words exchanged, he had known the dark girl shared his utter concentration in the search.

He reached a hand to Nora's arm and shook her gently till she opened her eyes.

"Better start watching," he told her.

"Vince, I'm scared." Her voice, raised over the engine

din, was harsh and half a scream. "Suppose something goes wrong? If we have to go down . . ."

"Forget about that," he told her grimly. "We won't be setting down. Not unless we spot them." They were heading up Seahhost Inlet now, low over gray water that showed its teeth to the hounding wind. A seaplane down in that welter of tide rips and pyramidal seas would be capsized in seconds. Rain rattled like shot against the windshield. Ardagh, fighting their drift, raised his voice. "That side is yours. I can't cover it, Nora. Watch! Don't quit watching!"

He lifted the mike and sent out his call letters again, tolling Grady at Quartz Harbor. But this time there was only the chatter and whine and slate-pencil yammer of static. Down there the northward-moving front had struck. They were on their own now, cut off, out of radio contact. Now no voice, no authority on earth could recall him.

He looked again at Nora. She had turned from him and was peering down through the starboard window. The cockpit was hot and stuffy, but her shoulders shook as if from bitter cold.

OF COURSE SHE LOVED HER CHILDREN. THE THINGS WES HAD said to her yesterday had been cruelly uncalled for. She did love them—she had suffered dreadfully to bear them, she had been a conscientious mother to them in every way.

But all her life she had made it her firm practice to accept facts, and no amount of weeping was going to bring Donald and Janet back. Finding the wrecked plane wouldn't do that. It would only add horror to a bereaved mother's load of grief. She hoped now, self-pity compounding her terror, that Flight Three would never be found.

They were all against her—Wes who of all people should be on her side—Vince who was acting like a madman and was going to kill them both—the unsympathetic reporters who were constantly trying to trip and confuse her with sly questions, as if a busy and successful woman could possibly know to the last finicking detail what her children wore.

She had counted on Wes, and what ailed him now she couldn't for the life of her understand. For all his fuss when the photographer sneaked that picture, she had a strong feeling Wes was secretly pleased.

"That does it, Nora," he had told her, standing over her with the newspaper crumpled in his fist. "That takes the ball right away from us. We've got to go along with Ardagh."

"I won't!" she had protested. "Wes, you saw his face, his eyes. I think he's crazy. I think . . ."

"Crazy, hell," Wes had told her. "He's a dozen times smarter than you are. I have to confess he even outsmarted me on that play. Now look. You're free of your kids, or will be soon. So you don't have to sit here making wax images and sticking 'em with pins any more. I'm going to level with you, Miss Stead. I'm going to be frank, utterly frank. You're on the skids. Not too far yet,

135

but one more box-office flop, one more stinker like your last, will send you down the slide. Play this right and you're in again. They'll have to hand you a decent role. It doesn't matter that you can't act worth a damn and never could act. The kind of publicity you'll get out of this will set you up better than you ever were. That's why I say, tag along with Ardagh. Fly on one trip with him. There won't be another—I guarantee that."

She had thought him in love with her. Now he was trying to get rid of her.

"I won't, Wes! I can't! I tell you, you don't know him."

"Oh, yes, I do! I know you too, darling, much too well." He was drunk enough to be ugly; he had squeezed her shoulder so hard in his big paw then that the blue marks remained. "You'll go along with him or I'll bust you the same way I made you. Overnight. You won't even rate as much as a gate pass when we get through. You'll be the mother who ratted out on her children, see? The tag will stick. They'll hiss your pictures off the screen, Nora, the same folks who bawled into their beer for you last night. The studio will cut its losses on you, drop you like that!"

She had tried to fight back. "This is all your fault, Wes. You were so sure you could have those pictures killed! And you seem to forget I have a contract—"

He had made a vulgar noise in his throat.

"Nora, I used to believe you were a bright girl. Now I'm beginning to wonder. Let's not have any false sentiment about this. You snatched the kids from Ardagh because you thought they'd be nice little background props. I didn't agree. You've been stuck with them ever since, as we both very well know. For a while longer you'll stay stuck with them. If you refuse, the ash can's open for you, and so help me, it's Wes Connor will toss you in."

He had won, of course. If he hadn't won she would not be here, flying in a storm with a lunatic beside her, her life in peril from moment to moment.

The shallow, erratic mind, steadfast only in ambition, doubled on its tracks like a creature pursued. Wes was wrong, they were all wrong. She loved the children, she did, she did!

For the time it took the seaplane to battle across a chain of spruce-dark ridges she clung to the role, the devoted mother braving all danger for her children's sake.

The plane rocked sickeningly, and she was Nora Stead again, the girl who meant to be somebody big, someone rich and famous, who had seized every slender chance and made the most of it, closing each compartment of her life behind her and never looking back. Only now the bulkheads were broken. The past had flooded through to the present. If there had been no children she would have been safe. There she had erred, and the error was about to kill her.

The terrible ridges, spiky with black spears of treetops, drifted beneath the floats. Ahead, a gray slope broke out of the rain, sweeping up in masses of shattered rock until the clouds swallowed it. She could look no longer. If she did she would be sick. If he forced her to keep on looking she would lose her reason.

Slowly, cautiously, she turned her head. He sat hunched and grim and unshaven in his filthy jacket that smelled of grease and dog, staring through the streaming windshield with red-rimmed eyes. He was a maniac with room for but one delusion in his twisted mind. She doubted if he even remembered now that she was with him in the plane.

Furtively, her hand stole to the pocket of the borrowed coat. Her fingers closed around the bottle, worked the top loose. She shook two of the powerful tablets into her palm. Twisting around as if to peer back into the cabin, Nora gulped the tablets.

She was asleep, arm on the window sill, chin on arm, when the Viking swept low over a dark valley with a rock slide at its head—a valley in which a lone pond lay like a staring eye, gray beneath the rain.

They had crossed the West Arm and were beating back along the sector when fog began to move in from the ocean before a shifting wind. In ten minutes, foothills and valleys were blanketed. That meant an end to contact flying.

Ardagh lifted the Viking until, at just over eight thousand, they broke through into clear sunlight. East beyond the shrouded Vancouver Island ranges, the peaks of the British Columbia mainland marched against a satin sky.

They could haul in their storm warnings for a while. The front which had swept northwest off the mainland was moving out to lose itself in the Pacific—the weather over these mountains was local, and would very easily break before morning.

Anyway, the day hadn't been entirely wasted. He was pretty sure now that the wreckage of Flight Three lay in none of the valleys they had covered, but higher up somewhere, close under the peaks.

It had been tricky work, and dangerous, since at no time had their altitude been sufficient to insure a water landing in case of trouble. Nora had borne up well, though, after that first flurry of panic. He felt a kindness toward her, a deeper warmth than he had known for a long time. He'd got into the habit of believing the children a poor second to Nora's career; but the way she had handled herself today gave the lie to that.

In two hours, she hadn't changed position. Ardagh looked at her where she huddled against the window with her face turned from him.

"Nora," he called. And when she didn't turn or answer, "I'm heading in. We'll be down in an hour."

Still she did not respond. He reached out and took her by the shoulder, shaking gently at first, then harder. Nora sighed, and sagged away from the window. Her eyes were closed.

Asleep?

God damn it, no!

He continued to shake her, and when that failed to rouse her, slapped her twice in hard, swinging cuffs. She whimpered and sighed again, and her eyes opened. Her face was dazed and blank.

Ardagh lifted his voice over the uneven noise of the engine, driving words at her harshly.

"How long, Nora?"

The red lips parted. She said dreamily, "Does it matter? They're dead, Vince. They've been dead for days, the

139

poor little things. I know it. Wes knows it. Everyone knows it but you, Vince. I was sure from the start."

He stared at her, listening to that soft and drowsy mumble.

"I didn't want to come. I knew it was useless. But Wes said people would talk if I didn't, and I had to come. Now I don't care any more. I'm going to sleep and sleep, and when I wake up it will all be over. . . ."

She was a child still, a spoiled and selfish child in an adult body. She had given him Don and Janet and taken them away, and now she had lost any claim to them. If he found them alive, if the Lord was that good to him, no power on earth would take them from him again.

Her eyes had closed. He studied the drugged and foolishly-smiling face he once had loved, then turned away, knowing that from this at least, he was forever free.

Almost kindly he said to her, "Nora, I think you're right. This isn't the place for you. I'll see that you and your friend have seats on the next ship out."

"He isn't my friend, Vince." She spoke without opening her eyes. "He's my husband. He has been for a year." Her shoulders settled deeper into the seat. "Poor Vince. I do believe you thought I'd come back to you!"

But her words scarcely reached him. The depression that settled upon him, black and bitter, stemmed from another cause. The morning's work was wasted, the children's chances fined down by that many more lost hours. Tagish would have been more use as a spotter. He should have brought Tagish—he should have brought Jule Thorne, not just her blue coat.

JANET WAS UNHAPPY AGAIN, MAYBE BECAUSE HE HAD scolded her last night for eating all the sandwiches but more likely because it was raining and she had wakened with a cold in her nose. She had gone back to being a baby. In the hours since what should have been breakfast time he had only managed to coax, lead and carry her a very little way down the creek.

It wasn't that she wanted to stop and play any more. She was nappy and squeaked her thumb most of the time, looking at him as if she didn't see him, her eyes no longer light hazel with little green flecks, but a darker brown and larger than they should be. It seemed to Don, trying to raise her from the damp moss of their latest resting place, that her face was thinner, too.

He shouldn't have scolded her about the sandwiches. You couldn't expect Janet to understand about anything like that. He had come down from setting the gully on fire and found her still tethered to her root, crumbs on her mouth and waxed paper around her, tossing crusts to a pair of jays that watched from a bush.

It wasn't much of a scolding and he hadn't slapped her hands as he had been minded to do when the enormity of Janet's act first burst upon him. He had stopped being hungry himself, and in a way he was glad his sister had eaten the last of their food. She had sung to herself quite happily while he pulled dry sticks from the top of a tiny log jam down the creek and carried them back to the hemlock's shelter.

Making the fire had been fun, even though most of the waxed paper was gone before the twigs caught. It was something like tea and coffee—a thing forbidden to children. But when the flames were climbing and the heavier wood began to crackle, Don felt a new confidence rise within him.

The fire made a tremendous difference. It laughed at the shadows and chased them back. It turned the hemlock trunk rosy and made the cove between the roots a snug shelter. While he bathroomed Janet and readied her for bed, she kept talking about a dog that had come and taken care of her while he was away.

He indulged her, saying, "That's nice," and, "What did the doggy tell you?" Little kids were funny. He was sure she had been too small to remember Tagish from their last visit with Dad, but here she was chattering about him as if she'd seen him just a while ago.

The feeling that something watched them didn't return. He guessed they had left the kelpy behind. The odd, hair-prickling sensation had worried him a lot—he could admit that, now it was gone.

The wet chunks from the lower part of the jam burned slowly. When they woke to the whisper of rain in the branches, a curl of smoke still rose from the blackened ends among the ashes. Don poked the fragments together, then fed in twigs and hunkered down to blow till the friendly flames were dancing again.

He was tempted to stay in this place, to keep the fire burning and wait till Dad landed and came up for them.

142

But reaching the pond in the valley had become an obsession with the little boy now. If they went on down to the pond it would mean they'd be with Dad that much sooner. Anyway, he had the cigarette lighter and when they got there he could make another fire.

Even then he might have stayed, for his sister's sake. But when he splashed out to mid-creek to get a drink for Janet in the hunting cap, he saw in the sand of the bar opposite something that pulled him up short.

If a man had pressed his fist, knuckles down, into the sand, he would have made marks like that. But if a man had been here he wouldn't just have made silly marks and gone on. Janet had talked about a dog last night. This wasn't a dog track either, or a bear's. It was the wrong shape. But if the kelpy had been around in the night, he was sure he would have known. Even in sleep, he would have felt it watching them.

So it had been here, but while Janet was alone, and it had looked like a big dog, even though its track seemed more of a cat-foot shape.

Don puzzled over the matter, scowling at the prints, till he looked around and saw Janet poking at the fire, and hurried back to her.

"What did the doggy do, baby?" he asked her.

"Sat." Her voice was rustier than ever from her cold. She had been sucking her thumb again; she took it from her mouth now, and pointed toward the creek. "The nice doggy sat there."

"What did the doggy look like, Janet?"

"Like a pussycat."

The thing baffled him. All he could be sure of was

that the kelpy had come and sat and watched her, and gone away. Maybe the fire and the explosion had scared it away.

It was the kelpy tracks as much as the advantages of being at the pond when Dad came that made him decide to go on. Janet asked for milk, but he could tell she had stopped expecting to get any. They breakfasted on the damp crusts Don had rescued from the whisky-jacks, then he buttoned his station-wagon coat around Janet, set the red hunting cap on her tangled curls, and rolled the blankets. The country looked easier ahead, and this time the blankets must go with them. Yesterday he had left Janet alone again. There had been no choice. But if the kelpy returned, he meant to be there with the detective's little blue gun in his hands.

Janet went along well enough, although slowly, until they came to a place where the creek dropped into a cleft between steep and slippery rocks. They couldn't go down, so they would have to take to the woods that crowded close on either side. It looked nice in the woods, not too tangled with brush, and the treetops would break the cold rain.

"Come on, Janet," he said, and reached for her scratched and mosquito-bitten hand. She pulled away and sat down. Her face puckered, her mouth squared, and Don knew if he kept on she was going to cry.

He released her hand and squatted on his heels beside her, and at once she leaned against him and began to squeak her thumb. That worried him. They'd only nicely got started—it was far too early for her nap. The silent friendly birds had tagged them from the last sleeping place, flitting from bush to bush. It was the birds that got Janet up and moving again at last. She watched them until they set her laughing, and when they moved on, she wanted to follow.

Don lifted her under her arms and she didn't make herself limp and heavy this time. As he had suspected, the trees made a good rainbreak. It seemed to him, too, that the mountain was becoming much less steep. Perhaps they really were near the pond now.

They emerged to an open place, a mossy tabletop where the trees thinned to make room for a bulge of rock. Don let Janet sit down while he unrolled the blankets and arranged her a nest. It was raining still, and even with the station-wagon coat, Janet had got herself wet from the creek. Her shoes were soaked and one of them had started to come apart, and her diaper was wet again, too.

He had saved most of his share of the sandwich crusts and now offered two of them to Janet, but she shook her head and pushed them away. Although he had a stomach ache and wasn't at all hungry, Don considered eating the crusts himself. He held them in his hand for a long time while he stood ankle-deep in the spongy moss, the rain darkening his hair, flattening all but the tuft of his rebellious crown.

Finally he returned the crusts to his side pocket, the one that didn't hold the gun and cigarette lighter.

It startled him to discover he hadn't once looked for the Viking since they left the foot of the rock slide. Janet was asleep. He arranged a fold of the blanket over her face, then, wrapped and hooded in the third blanket, settled himself on the bluff beside her to watch for Dad.

145

The little boy couldn't remember how long it was since the plane had gone bouncing and crashing down the mountainside. A long time ago, almost forever. All he knew for sure was that sometime, anytime, he would hear the drone in the sky, see the black speck growing larger till it took shape and color, and know Dad was coming to take them away.

He thought about it, the sound, the picture, growing plain, even plainer than it had been on the slope above the gully. But it wasn't inside his head, it was outside. This time it was more than just a dream-picture of what he wanted most in the world to see. It was as he had dreamed it—but it wasn't a dream, *it wasn't a dream.*

The humming was there, deepening to a triumph song in his ears. The black speck was visible below the clouds, growing larger, no longer a speck but a toy plane, a seaplane, a yellow seaplane rushing down upon them with its floats reaching eagerly like slender silver feet.

The Viking swept over. In the instant of its passing, Don saw the black letters on its blunt wing and Dad's bright red triangle on the fuselage. He saw a face, a woman's white face that gazed down upon him. Motionless, held in a paralysis of joy, he watched the seaplane bore low over a timbered shoulder and out of his sight. He could no longer see the pond for the cloud tatters that drifted below, but it was down there in the woods somewhere, winking its friendly eye. Dad would have spotted it. He would be circling back toward it now. In no time at all he would bring the Viking in over the trees that ringed it.

Don stood over his sister, blanket thrown aside, oblivi-

146

ous of the rain that trickled down his neck. The engine noise wasn't even a pulse in the air any more. They were down. Dad had landed.

Waking Janet was hard. Even when he had laced her boots, making a slow job of it because of the trembling of his fingers, she kept on crying and doing her best to burrow into the blankets. Talking to her didn't help. At last he wrapped his arms around her middle and with Janet kicking and howling, staggered down from the low bluff with her. It didn't matter about the blankets now, or about them having no food and being soaked and torn and cold. None of that mattered, now the Viking had arrived.

He toiled in a joyful kind of nightmare. He carried Janet until the world of dark, scaly tree trunks swam around him and he had to drop with her and lie gasping till his strength and wind returned. When his legs would again bear his weight, he hauled her on, down through the forest until the creek was once more chuckling close beside them.

"Not far now, baby," he panted to Janet. "Only a little way. You try to walk. Help Donnie!"

She was a good baby, the best little sister in the world. She croaked around her thumb, "Help Donnie," and struggled to her feet and tottered on with the hunting cap jammed forward on her head and the quilted coat trailing at her heels.

It was a travesty of progress. The sole of Janet's broken boot had torn loose and flapped at every step. It tripped her, and she fell and rolled into a hole between down logs, helpless in the bulky coat. Don tugged his handkerchief from his hip pocket. He dragged Janet out of the hole and tied the rag around her boot. The ends stuck up in twin tufts and he said to her, "Look, Janet! Rabbit's ears!"

That pleased her. She got up, and they pushed on, Don straining for a glimpse of the pond's gray eye, Janet snuffling along, thumb in mouth, watching the rabbit ears.

The rain no longer sifted through the treetop canopy. The woods changed, the ground leveling, the dark trunks drawing farther apart. Ahead, only a little way ahead, Don caught the dulled gleam of water. They rounded a great, mossy boulder, and the mountain released them.

They stood amid brush that came to Janet's neck, at the edge of a tiny meadow. Below the meadow was the pond, wind-ruffled, marshy at its edges, its waters more brown than gray.

The pond was empty. The Viking hadn't landed.

Realization knocked him stupid. Don stood staring while Janet found a clear place and plumped down to play with the rabbit ears. Dad must have seen them! The woman with the white face pressed to the window had been looking directly at them. But they hadn't landed, they had flown away.

He began to cry then, not with his eyes but deep inside, a child punished cruelly and beyond all reason. The pond in the valley had meant everything toward which they had struggled—Dad to take care of them, milk to drink, dry clothes, warmth, food, and beyond all else, someone to help with Janet. They had reached the pond and it was empty, ugly, no longer winking at them in friendship. They stood by the pond and they had less than they had started out with. This time he couldn't go back for the blankets.

The feeling of being watched cut through to him, sudden and strong. He whirled, looking back on the way they had come. The merest twitch of movement drew his gaze to the boulder that humped where the woods broke to the brush. Something crouched there, tawny-gray and motionless now, as if the rock itself had altered shape.

This was the kelpy. This was the thing that had screamed in the night and left its tracks on the creek bar. This mask that peered at them, this cat face thrust over the boulder, was the very face of his fear.

The dark spell snapped. He drew the gun from his pocket, raised it in both hands, pointed it at the face and squeezed the trigger. He squeezed four times, seeing moss and stone chips fly, hearing over the loud explosions the wail of a deflected bullet through the timber.

The boulder was as it had been when they passed it first. The Halloween mask had dissolved, vanished.

Soberly, Don looked down at the gun in his hands. There had been three explosions, but when he pressed the trigger the fourth time, only a click. The bullets were all gone, the gun was no more use to him.

Janet was tumbling and squealing in the brush. He recovered her and lugged her out to the open meadow. He was trembling now, and his arms and legs felt weak as if there was no muscle in them. There were no such things as kelpies, Dad had told him that. The face so like a mask pulled taut over short, square muzzle and flat skull belonged to a cougar, and it was the great cat's hateful, furtive presence he had felt on the rock slide yesterday, with a prickling of his hair.

Nora had seen them. He didn't think Nora cared very much about them, but she'd tell Dad, and he would come back. Until then he must not sleep or even close his eyes. He must light a fire and build it high, and above all else, he must not leave Janet alone for a moment.

THE HAND THAT RULED SEAHHOST VILLAGE BELONGED NOT to Chief Koskima, that tough and ancient pagan, but to a roly-poly priest who cruised the inlets with a Saint Christopher's medal nailed to his mast and thirty feet of teredo-riddled hull beneath him. Father Jerome sat this drizzling afternoon in Alex Prince's kitchen, one ear tuned to his host's conversation, the other cocked for stirrings in the back bedroom. Chuck-Charley Koskima was sleeping off a loganberry jag in there, having been kicked out of his grandfather's house after two days of scandalous drunkenness.

For his own as well as Chuck-Charley's sake, Father Jerome hoped the demon would soon release its grip. He was immobilized here at Seahhost with a leaky gland and a bent propeller shaft, result of a scrape with a reef, and although Chuck-Charley was a back-slidden young scoundrel, God had seen fit to give him a knack for things mechanical.

"So that's how it was, Fadder," he heard Alex Prince

say. "Me, I'm so surprised to see that old one-eyed . . . fella down this way, I just stand there wit' my mouth hanging open. When I do toss a shot after him, he's in the timber and all I get is a patch of fur."

Alex had been yarning about cougar. The corpulent old hunter was almost unique among his coast-hugging people in his love for the inland woods. In his time he had bagged something over a hundred of the great cats, and Father Jerome was beginning to feel that he, personally, had been in at the death of each.

He said now, reasonably sure of his ground, "You pursued the beast, Alex?"

"No. I would of, but my missus, she put her foot down. She tells me I'm too old for siwashing around in de woods." His heavy laugh rumbled out. "Ever since, I've been frettin' about that cat. I know him from away back; me and him is old friends, you might say. He's a screamer, the only one I ever heard, or heard tell of. Twice I've heard him scream, years apart. He's killed three good dogs on me, and I've yet to see him in a tree."

"Extraordinary!" Father Jerome murmured. He wasn't sure, but thought he heard a groan from the back room. Perhaps Chuck-Charley wouldn't keep him waiting much longer.

"Fadder, what would you say about a cat that walks all round a man asleep, close enough to look in his face?"

"Why," the priest replied, "if the man happened to be Alex Prince, I'd say the cat was rash to the point of being suicidal."

"He was daring me. That's what. Just like he dared me

last week when he showed up by the kids' swimming hole."

"Did he do that?" Father Jerome straightened a little in his chair, Chuck-Charley and the gasboat for the moment forgotten.

"Sure, just like I told you a minute ago! There he sat, not two hundred yards from where the kids was yelling and splashing."

"Such a creature should be destroyed with no more delay than need be," Father Jerome declared with conviction. "It's a great pity you missed him, Alex."

"Yeah. I been kicking myself ever since. One day that devil is going to come back, and just maybe I'm not there wit' the rifle."

It was the little priest's private opinion that any cougar bold enough to dare Seahhost's juvenile population would emerge the loser, but at the same time he recognized a potential menace, and his interest in his charges was practical as well as spiritual. Also, experience had taught him to see beneath the surface of the old hunter's words.

"Had it occurred to you that you might forestall the unpleasant possibility?"

"You mean go after 'im?" His host spoke with ill-concealed eagerness.

"Exactly."

"The wife would t'row a fit. Anyhow, it's the wrong time of year, no snow. Still, he's old and slowed up, and the woods is wet. I guess my dogs could use a workout too, so fat and lazy they're getting. . . ."

"And Alex Prince stands in need of a holiday," the

152

priest finished for him, smiling as he exposed the root of the matter.

"That's a fact! Things here has got me so I couldn't tell you which end is which! My Norma, she's taken it in her head to marry that young no-good in yonder, and the old lady is on their side. I tell you, Fadder, I'm a lot better off in the woods!"

Father Jerome said mildly, "I will so point out to Mrs. Prince when she returns, if you wish."

"Thanks!" Alex leaped from his chair with a boy's alacrity. "After the scare I give him, he'll be back in his proper range, away upriver toward the high country. I've got a line cabin and grub cache at the Forks. I can make the cabin by dark and see can the dogs cut his trail tomorrow. And even if we don't find him, there's a couple young cats I know of in back."

"Excellent," said Father Jerome. He had read somewhere that an attack by a cougar upon a human was practically unknown, but having seen many a probability upset in his years along the coast, he was chary of sweeping judgments. "But after what you've told me, I'd suggest you concentrate on the one-eyed gentleman."

Alex Prince, the priest knew, was quite capable of pulling a longbow about the swimming hole incident for the sake of clerical support. With him out of the way, however, the women of his house could lead Chuck-Charley into marriage without interference from one notoriously bullheaded. A good wife might be just what young Koskima needed to ballast him.

Gravely but with an inward smile, he watched from the doorway a scant ten minutes later as Alex strode from his

153

cluttered yard with his two hounds sedate at the heels of his stitch-broken cruisers and his three mongrels frolicking before him.

"Good hunting, my son," he called, and got a grin and a lift of Alex's rifle as the rain-drenched spruce forest swallowed him.

The hum of an airplane came to Father Jerome from high overhead. He peered up, the drizzle wetting his cheeks, but saw nothing save a ceiling of cloud broken by a lone patch of blue. It was a poor day for flying, and he wished the unknown pilot well. He might be one of the men who, his gasboat radio had told him, sought that other plane, the lost one. He had been strongly moved as he listened; and the picture of the young father who would not believe his children dead returned to touch the priest's kind old heart now. An allegory there . . . the stuff from which a telling sermon might be woven.

"Good hunting!" Father Jerome muttered again, this time to the invisible plane whose uneven engine sound was now diminishing south across Seahhost Inlet. The words were a wish and a blessing.

Behind him, he heard a second, louder groan, and the thud of booted feet hitting the floor. He turned, his expression firming to severity. Chuck-Charley had shaken off his loganberry stupor at last. The gasboat lay in stinking low-tide mud; for one in Chuck-Charley's condition, straightening her shaft and repacking the gland would be penance enough.

JULE SAT WITH RICK HYATT ON THE DEACONS' BENCH OUTSIDE the radio-telephone shack, looking moodily down to a harbor now almost empty of planes and fishboats. It was well past noon, her breakfast had consisted of a cup of lukewarm coffee, but she wasn't at all hungry. Ardagh and Nora Stead had been out something better than five hours, and except for one call forty minutes after they left Quartz Harbor, the pilot hadn't been heard from.

"Quit fussing," Rick Hyatt told her. "Anyone'd think you were married to the guy."

"I'm not fussing. I just wish they'd check in, that's all. Vince Ardagh is my assignment."

"That," Hyatt said dryly, "is one of the better known facts of this metropolis." He studied his camera critically, turning it in his hands. "You know, Connor would be writing it on fences, if they had fences up here. You should have attended his press conference this morning."

"Did you?"

"For laughs, yeah. The keynote was co-operation. We'd all do so much better if we didn't try to cut each other's throats. A reporter who wouldn't play ball was as much a danger to the common cause as a rogue pilot who upset the search plan by flying off in all directions. He was going to issue a statement, but someone started a rumor the beer parlor was open, and we adjourned. All except your

155

man, Thorson. He and Connor had their heads together when I left."

"What about?" She wasn't much interested. Thorson seemed to have got over his mad, and the Atlas-International director hadn't entered her thoughts since last night.

"You could ask Thorson. You're on the same paper, aren't you?"

She didn't answer, and Hyatt chuckled, turning his camera in freckled hands. "Thorson drifted in here while you were up seeing the fat guy, what's-his-name, Ardagh's pal. Beer don't agree with me, so I tagged him. He put in a call to McDevitt."

She was listening now, half-turned on the bench and giving the thick-set photographer her full attention.

"Sure, I kibitzed," Hyatt told her. "From what I heard, it looks like two things. First, Thorson was squealing to teacher, and second, your assignment has folded."

"What do you mean?"

"They're fixing to ground him."

"Ardagh? They couldn't."

"No? I checked it with Grady, and he tells me they not only can, they're going to." Hyatt tipped his head toward the hotel. "Connor gets part credit for that. He beefed to the Air Regulations watchdog about Ardagh risking Miss Glamour's neck in an unsafe plane, and threatened to wire Ottawa if Langmuir didn't do something to stop him. Langmuir's a good little guy, but he's D.O.T. to his backbone. Anyhow, Ardagh ought to be grounded. He's punchy, he's walking on his heels."

Jule considered Hyatt's news with sinking heart. On

the ground, out of the search, Ardagh would crack up. In his dreadful singleness of purpose, the search was his alone. She had come to share that feeling—if Flight Three was to be found, it was Ardagh who would find it.

Hyatt said, "He kept me awake most of the night. Ardagh, I mean. My room's next to his, and that joint has plywood walls. Along about two in the morning, he begun groaning and talking in his sleep. Then he rolled out and paced the floor for a couple of hours." He made a minute adjustment to his flash-gun synchronizer. "God hates a floor-pacer. I'd a lot sooner he snored."

"How do you expect him to sleep?"

"You know," the *Herald* photographer said thoughtfully, "you can't always be right. The other night I as much as told Ardagh he was a phony. He'd blocked me on a shot I needed, and him taking a poke at me didn't help, either."

"But you got your picture," Jule said.

"Sure. He made me give him the film pack, but I pulled a gypsy switch on him and slipped him a blank. I figured the thing in this for him and the pin-up girl was publicity, that they didn't give a damn about those kids. About her, I haven't changed my mind."

"Ardagh doesn't care about publicity," Jule said. Her words were those Brandreth had used to her, what now seemed an eternity ago. "He doesn't know any of us are alive, Rick."

"He knows you're alive. He talked about you in his sleep. You and them. His kids. It was creepy, listening to him, especially when you've got a family yourself."

Stretching and yawning, Hyatt got up. "Him and that

157

dog of his. The dog's another floor-pacer. Just look at him."

Tagish was coming down from the direction of the hotel. He paced in the middle of the street, a dignified and lonely dog, and a patently unhappy one. A wirehair dashed from the general store to challenge him, but maintained a respectful distance, and the Doberman padded on with never a side glance.

"He was moping around the floats all morning," Hyatt said. "That's where he's headed now, I guess."

Jule got up too. The sound in her ears wasn't merely the product of wishful thinking.

"You and the dog," Hyatt said. "I don't hear anything."

"There's a plane coming in."

The photographer listened with mouth open. "Yeah.... Now I got it." His grin was friendly. "It's your man's bucket of bolts. Only one ship around here sounds like that."

Tagish had quickened his pace to a lope. They followed him, picking their way along the plank street on boards that wabbled beneath them in liquid mud. The seaplane was in sight now, dropping low over the north ridge.

"Jeez," Hyatt said. "Listen to her! Once Langmuir gets his paws on her she'll be grounded like he'd sawed the wings off her."

The Viking sideslipped down to land close in. She taxied to the landing with a rough roaring. Hyatt reached for the wing tip. Ardagh got out, ducked under, and opened the right-hand door. He reached for Nora Stead's arm. She alighted clumsily, and would have toppled from the float but for the pilot's grip. He landed her without a word spoken. There was something entirely impersonal about the act; Nora Stead could have been no more than any routine passenger ticketed for Quartz Harbor.

He was in bad shape. Jule watched him anxiously as he made fast. His movements were fumbling and slow. When he straightened and turned, the face with the squinted eyes and the harsh lines from nostrils to mouth corners looked more tired, older than she had remembered.

"No luck?" Jule asked him.

He shook his head. "We'll give it a try later, if you're up to it."

Nora Stead was unbuckling the blue coat. Neither Ardagh nor the photographer moved to help her. She took the coat off, folded it, and held it out to Jule.

"Thanks," she said thickly. "Thanks a lot." The hint of music, the intimate, mellow quality was gone from her voice. She looked ill and middle-aged, and she moved as she had in the Hotel Maquinna lobby, as if she walked in her sleep.

Nora passed them, stumbling toward the gangplank. Rick Hyatt ambled after her, swinging his Graflex and whistling softly to himself.

"What happened, Vince?"

"Nothing. We ran into a little weather." He stood frowning, rubbing the Doberman's head. "What about it, Jule? Will you come up later?"

"Of course." There was no point in telling him what had been done to him. He'd hear about that soon enough, from Grady or the inspector.

Bill Grady was standing in the doorway of the radio shack, tall in flight jacket and blue uniform slacks, his line cap pushed back on his dark hair.

"Inside a minute, eh, Vince?" he said, and Ardagh followed him through.

Jule returned to her bench-warming. She lit a cigarette; she felt jumpy and tense, almost frightened. She didn't know what she had expected—a row, perhaps a major blowup—but Ardagh's voice was no more audible than the search captain's.

It didn't take long. Her cigarette wasn't a third smoked when Ardagh came out. He said to her in a flat and quiet voice, "The trip's off, Jule," and started down the steps, Tagish at his side.

"Wait!" He was taking it too quietly. A blowup would have been a lot better. She looked down at him where he stood in the planked street. "Vince, they're right. If you keep on, you'll kill yourself. You're not alone on it, you know. Most of the other planes are up now."

"Sure," he said. "So Grady told me. Sure, everything's dandy." His eyes scared her. He said in the same flat voice, "I didn't tell you, did I, kid? She knocked herself out. She slept for three hours, the only three hours when we might have spotted them. When she woke up she told me they were dead. Everyone knows it but me, huh?"

"No! I don't know that. I don't believe it, Vince."

"We're a minority, Jule. They're dead, all right." He peered up at her, the old-man's face strange under the fine, light hair. "You know what I'm going to do?"

"Go to the hotel. Lie down and get some sleep. Maybe tomorrow—"

"I'm going to hold a wake," the pilot said. "That's what. I'm going to hold the longest, loudest one-man wake this town has ever seen. Then I'm going to beat hell out of a puffball called Connor." He was rocking gently on his heels, hands shoved into his pockets. The bloodshot eyes burned in the drawn face. "You're a sweet girl, Jule. Cry for them, will you? I can't."

She watched them in deep distress, man and lank black-and-tan dog, as they plodded off along the muddy street. When the hotel door closed on them she crossed the verandah and entered the office. The operator gave her his friendly nod. Grady, scowling over maps on the table, did not look up.

She knew more about the tall, quiet search chief than she had when he blew in that morning. He had been a bush pilot, John Brandreth had told her, and his glacier and river bar landings had made him a legend in Alaska. For a time she had thought him over-cautious in his refusal to send up other aircraft; but as visibility improved and the gale threat lifted, he had dispatched ship after ship. Nine float planes were now strip-patterning the sections north of Quartz Harbor which Grady had assigned their pilots. Four other bush jobs were running down new leads received from scattered points on the coast. A light-keeper at Folly Point had sighted floating wreckage which could be from a plane. South on Nyall River, an isolated logging crew had heard something big go over, low and with limping engines, three nights past. One of the two amphibians was hunting an area thirty miles offshore where a salmon troller had dragged his lines yesterday through an oil slick several acres in extent.

The lead from the Seahhost Aragon sector was now only one of many. But Grady was keeping his thumb firm on that one. The U.S. Coast Guard Grumman could hold the air longer than any other of the search craft. Grady had sent it north on the heels of the weather to scout every foot of that difficult territory not blanked out by fog.

The search was running smoothly and efficiently, but Jule felt with a leaden hopelessness that it was all to no purpose. She had made Ardagh believe, and his belief had swept her along by its white intensity. He had stopped believing now, and the thing was finished.

If Flight Three were down in the mountains, they'd find her some day or some year and do what they had to do—fetch out the bodies or bury them at the scene of the crash. Thirty-six adults, and a blond boy of eight, and a girl not yet three, with curly brown hair, and a Teddy bear she called Anna.

It wasn't her affair, she told herself savagely. She was not personally concerned, and it was worse than silly to let herself get maudlin over it. She had come in here with a notion no less silly. There was no use trying to enlist Grady's help for Vince Ardagh. The D.O.T. inspector wouldn't set a man down without ample cause, and once grounded, outside intercession was pointless. Langmuir's decision was sound, and would probably have been made even without Connor's interference. She could admit that now. If Ardagh was allowed to continue on the search, another crash would be the almost certain result.

McDevitt had summed it up in the newsroom when he grudgingly allowed her this assignment. In the broad picture, Ardagh and his troubles signified very little.

It was two o'clock. She ought to check with McDevitt. But she had nothing new, and the tears were close behind her eyes, so close that one shove from Mac would spill them.

"You waiting to make a call, miss?" the operator asked her.

She shook her head and went out, walking slowly down toward the landing where Grady's Fairchild and Ardagh's battered Viking sat alone at the float-string. On the way, she passed Inspector Langmuir striding briskly up from the dock with Ardagh's logbook under his arm.

Brandreth was not in sight. He hadn't slept at all well; she had left him lying down in the room he shared with the pilot. It was odd not to see the large, ungainly figure busy under the seaplane's engine cowling.

The sun came full out and warmed the weathered planks. Jule spread her coat in a cove amid boxes of freight and lay there with her profitless thoughts circling her brain until the compounded weariness of the search sent her drifting into sleep.

John Brandreth trudged down alone, late in the afternoon, and found her there. The big man stood over her, knuckles on hips, the wind ruffling his sparse, sandy hair. His ugly face was soft as if he looked down at a sleeping child. He moved a box, cautiously, to make shade for the girl's head, then tramped on down the float-string to the

Viking. Grounding the Captain's ship had been easy as shooting fish in a basket. She was time-expired, a long way past the six hundred hours allowed her between major overhauls.

When Jule woke, the sun had rolled behind the westward ridges and the evening silence was beginning to throb to the pulse of homing aircraft. Alone on the floatstring, she upended a crate and sat on it, and for the next hour, brooding there, watched them drop one by one over the hills—the helicopter up from Washington State, the bush jobs, the ships of the Royal Canadian Air Force. The U.S. Coast Guard amphibian came bumbling in latest of all the fleet, black and ungainly against an apple-green sky in which the first star showed. She moored among the graceful trollers. Her crew pulled ashore in a rubber dinghy.

The lieutenant-commander who skippered that ship gave Jule a nod and a smile as he passed.

"Anything new?" Jule asked him, and he told her, "Nothing."

Thorson had strolled down from the beer parlor. He stood by her now, jingling the change in his pockets. Presently he said, "So they shot your horse out from under you, Jule."

He spoke amiably, but she sensed in him a triumph not too well concealed.

"You know, honey," he said, "it would have been a lot better if Mac had got it from you. The way he split the story, Ardagh was your assignment, remember? When you didn't show up this morning, somebody had to phone it."

"That's all right, Bob. I didn't mind."

This handsome, lazily cynical reporter had impressed her once, although she had never truly liked him. Now he was a minor nuisance, of less consequence to her than the mosquitoes which evening had fetched in clouds from the dank woods.

"I don't like having to do McDevitt's hatchet work," he was saying now, "but it seems I'm tagged." He made a show of fumbling in his jacket pocket, and produced a folded sheet of copy paper.

"Here," he said. "Mac's compliments. I took it down verbatim."

She opened the note and glanced at the scribble with only faint curiosity. Thorson watched her, jingling his change.

Miss Thorne:

She could see the little man very plainly, calm amid the pre-deadline hustle, brain and hands busy with half a dozen emergencies.

As a woman, I esteem you. As a reporter, I find, regretfully, that objectivity is a virtue which you possess in even lesser degree than others of your sex. Since you have failed entirely to support your thesis, and since your protagonist has lost his tilt with the windmills, you can serve no useful purpose where you are. You will return on tonight's steamer, in a frame of mind suitable to covering the annual rally of the Daughters of Confederation, which I find open in my book.
Vae victis.

"The boat," Thorson said, "is due in around ten o'clock, they tell me."

You couldn't escape. You could tell yourself the gamble, the risks and the hurt were for others, and you could even come to believe it in time. But she knew, now, the answer to Brandreth's ruthless "Why?" of the other morning, and accepted it calmly, almost unconcernedly. When you stopped taking those risks, you stopped living.

"I won't be going back," she said to Thorson. "Tell McDevitt next time you call that he'll have to find someone else for his convention."

The vain and handsome man, the reporter who had nursed the sting of his injured vanity so lovingly, stared at her.

"Okay," he said. "I'll tell him. If he doesn't can you he'll toss you right back into social, you know. You take that boat, Jule, and I'll do my best to straighten it out with Mac."

He stood jingling his change a while longer, puzzled and disconcerted, then left her alone with the mosquitoes and the restless twilight whispering of the tide.

It wasn't just disappointment and exhaustion that had worked the change in Ardagh. She could only guess what had happened between him and Nora Stead, alone in the seaplane a hundred miles north. It was not a thing to be asked; perhaps if he wanted to, one day he would tell her.

She was in love with the pilot, and had been for some time—probably before ever this search began. She smiled to herself in the dusk, with a wry quirking of her lips. Vince Ardagh, right now, was a very poor gamble.

The beer parlor across from the general store was doing a roaring trade tonight. She wondered if he was in there. Not likely—his wouldn't be the sort of drinking that wanted company, and he would not be wasting his time on beer.

More as protection against the ravenous mosquitoes than for warmth, Jule shrugged into her coat. Something made a bump in the left-hand pocket. She tugged out a bottle of white tablets, the same bottle she had seen on Nora Stead's dresser last night. For a moment she studied it, the frown deepening between her eyes, then tossed it away from her, into the sea.

Frowning still, she turned and climbed up from the floats. She was off the dock and halfway to the hotel when the door of the radio shack banged open and two men exploded onto the verandah. A thunderous growling came to her through the night. She ran, slipping and staggering on the greasy corduroy—glimpsed a stiff-legged shadow at the edge of the tangle and, greatly daring, thrust her fingers through the Doberman's studded collar.

Wes Connor wabbled up from the mud. His checked shirt was ripped open from throat to belt, his hands were pushed out before him. He backed stumbling toward the doorway, his voice pitched high with terror:

"Grab him, somebody! Get him away from me! He's crazy!"

Ardagh came up off his knees. Hands snatched at him but he tore free, his own face blood-smeared, his fair hair tumbled over his eyes, and lunged at Connor. He caught the man in the doorway; Jule heard the meaty double-chop of his fists landing, saw Connor topple backward into the shack.

Bill Grady's uniform cap bobbed over the hurly-burly. He and the radio-telephone operator had Ardagh by the arms and were wrestling him away from Connor. Jule heard Rick Hyatt's voice in her ear, sharp and urgent.

"Better get him out of this! Thorson's gone for the town cop."

She released Tagish and pushed her way through the knot of men by the door.

"Let me," she said to Grady; and took Ardagh by the arm, swung him, and led him out of there.

He was drunk. He was very drunk. Brandreth should be here. She looked around for him, badly frightened and angry that Brandy hadn't taken the pilot in hand. Then, not finding that help, she started Ardagh down the street toward the inlet, away from the lights and the din of voices. He stumbled beside her, obedient to her hand.

"You know what he did, Jule?" he muttered thick-voiced. "You want to know? That God damn Connor. It was him got me grounded, he had them put me down. . . ."

On the dock, the town behind them, the pilot halted. He freed his arm and lurched around to face her.

"I'm on the beach," he told her, grinning, swaying a little, squinting at her through moonlight that whitened the dock. "But I'm not going to stay on the beach. Not me. It's a fine, fair night, Jule. I'll find them. I'm going north to find 'em."

"Vince, you can't!"

"I didn't feel right for a wake, Jule. Tomorrow we'll hold the wake. Not tonight. Tonight I've got business north."

He grinned at her and she was afraid of him suddenly, but more afraid for him. He said, "Not you, Jule. You're not going. I like you too much. Y'see, I'm a lost cause.

I'm the Flying Dutchman, didn't they tell you? Write that in your paper, sweetheart. Vince Ardagh, the hot pilot, the fireball. Only trouble with him, he's a Flying Dutchman, he flies and he flies and he'll keep on flying till hell freezes, but it won't ever get him anywhere."

"You can't do it, Vince." It was like bouncing words from a stone wall. "You're grounded, and you're in no condition to fly. Sit down here a while. Rest while I go and find Brandy."

He stepped past her. His voice came back to her, light now, almost gay. "About my wife, Jule. My ex-wife. You know her. A very beautiful woman, Nora Stead. She's psychic, I ever tell you that? Well, I'm psychic too. This is the night, Jule. Tonight I find 'em, tomorrow the wake."

She watched him jolt heavily down the gangplank and stride across to his seaplane. He knelt to the ringbolt, the shadow of the wing dark above him, unmoored, and dragged the Viking by her wing tip to the outer end of the float-string. He opened the cockpit door and clambered in. Tagish stood for a moment in moonlight, whining softly, then scrambled after him.

Jule called to him once, a wild, shrill cry, then ran down to the plane. As the propeller began to turn, she wrenched the door open and tumbled in. She sprawled against the Doberman. Tagish moved away, into the dark cargo space of the cabin. The engine's coughing deepened to uneven thunder. Jule settled into the right-hand seat, looking down through the window at pale wings of spray that ghosted up from the rushing pontoons. They missed a gasboat by inches. The seaplane came up on her steps and lifted clear, shivering, steadying as she rose. The pilot banked steeply over the harbor in a climbing turn.

Men were running down the dock. Jule saw those black and tiny figures for a moment, the moon-paled lights of the town behind them, then the Viking was over the northwest ridge and clawing into the sky. On their left lay a silver ocean upon which ghostly fog banks cruised, on their right loomed the steep, timbered buttresses and jagged peaks of the Island ranges.

A hand closed on her shoulder. She wrenched around, and saw a dim white moon of a face, heard a familiar heavy voice in her ear:

"Open your window."

"Brandy. How did you get here?"

"Hell, I knew he'd try it. Meant to stop him." He was leaning on the back of her seat; Jule felt the chuckle shake him. "But darn if I didn't go to sleep."

"What can we do, Brandy?"

"Stick with him, I guess, since he don't carry 'chutes. He's better drunk than most of 'em sober. Open that window, eh? Give him a shot of air."

She ought to be afraid. But she felt confident and oddly happy, her mind settled as if a heavy trouble had been lifted from her. She ran down the window on her side. The chill blast cut at her. Ardagh's head jerked back. He scrubbed a hand across his eyes in the familiar small-boy gesture, as if he were waking from deep sleep.

They flew over three deep and winding inlets. Ardagh banked to follow the course of the fourth, driving inland toward peaks whose crests were ringed by masses of pearly cloud. They were close to those peaks when without explanation he turned off course and put the Viking west again toward salt water.

While the inlet was still distant, the engine's growling roar was punctuated by a series of coughs. The silence that followed was terrifying.

Ardagh did not speak. His utter concentration beat back the panicky question that leaped to Jule's lips. A river twisted below. In this strange hush, Jule heard the mutter of its rapids, saw its pale strand slashing the moon-polished ebony of timber. They glided over it now, their angle of descent flattening. The river widened, branching and wandering in a multiplicity of channels. The reach below them was no longer silver but dark—to Jule, staring down, its surface was indistinguishable from the shadows flung across it. The seaplane's landing lights drowned in it without reflection.

For an instant they seemed to hover. Then the floats struck hard, obscuring the windows with sheets of spray. Something caught the plane and slewed her violently, almost capsizing her. She nosed over, folding the pilot across his steering column, jolting Jule forward so that the safety belt threatened to sever her middle.

They were down, and in one piece. She realized it in a dazed fashion, her eyes tear-filled from the pain of a bumped nose. Above her Ardagh said crankily, "Why the devil wasn't that belt cinched tight?"

He had been drunk when they left Quartz Harbor, but he seemed sober now, and apparently not greatly disconcerted by a landing which to her appeared just short of suicidal.

She said furiously, "Look! You've been taking it out on

171

everyone around you for days! The inspector did right to ground you! You shouldn't be allowed to fly . . ."

"Shut up!"

She slapped him, rocking his head back. Then she began to cry, her control breaking like a rotten twig.

She could feel Brandreth's hand patting her shoulder. He said to Ardagh, "I'm going to climb out for a look-see, Captain. At your age, I kind of figure a man should have the sense to keep an eye on his fuel gauge."

Ardagh let her cry. After a while he lit cigarettes, his face strangely relaxed, almost peaceful in the match flare. He gave her one of the cigarettes.

"I'm sorry, kid," he said. "Brandy's right. I'm the fool of the world." He drew on his cigarette, and said, "You know, the way we squabble, we ought to be married."

Nothing more for a long time. Jule found her handkerchief presently, and blew her nose. She had never gone hysterical before. The Viking was canted forward so that it was an effort to stay in the seat.

"I'm sorry, too. Do you think we can get out of here, Vince?"

"Sure."

"I mean the plane." Their search couldn't end ridiculously, like this.

"We'll get her off. . . . What about that, Jule?"

"About what?"

"Marrying me. It'd be strictly a long shot. I'm busted, but I'm over Nora. I think in time I'll pick myself up off my face."

She had wanted this—she knew she had wanted it more than anything in the world. But she only said in a voice as casual as the pilot's, "We'll talk about that later, Vince. After we've found them."

"Yes," he said. "After we've found them. You stay here. I'll take a line ashore."

Father Jerome's saints only interceded for him in major crises. This was a minor contretemps, no more than an absent-minded mistaking of a blind slough for the channel that corkscrewed out to tidehead from Seahhost Village. His mission boat had chugged around two bends, and he was beginning to wonder mildly why the channel had not yet opened to the ocean, when through the fog that had rolled in after moonset, he spied a yellow seaplane on a half-submerged mudbank dead ahead.

He peered at it in mounting concern as his boat closed the distance. Definitely not the plane they sought; that one, he knew from his radio, was a great silver ship with four engines. One of the searchers, then, perhaps the same one who had flown over the village yesterday, had come to grief here in Seahhost River estuary.

Relief set him smiling as he drew near enough to spot the line that stretched from the plane's tail to the bank of the slough. The mists swirled clear to reveal two men, one bulky, the other lean and fair-haired, sunk ankle-deep in mud. The figure behind them resolved itself from a boy badly in need of a haircut to a dark girl in slacks and a blue coat plastered with mud. There was also a dog.

The little priest hailed. The answering shout carried a warning.

"Better stand off! You'll be aground in a minute!"

From bitter experience, Father Jerome knew how tidal

mire could grip a hull. He ducked to the house and yanked his gears through neutral into reverse. The gasboat slowed, her abused engine thumping, then pulled stern-first away from the shallow. The priest was by this time aware that he had missed the channel. He backed till his boat had six feet of water beneath her, then cut his power and squirreled forward to drop anchor. Before he had his dinghy overboard, the blond man was wading out to him.

He was so wet, Father Jerome decided, that a further ducking wouldn't matter. An impetuous young man— he had reached deeper water and was swimming strongly now. The big black dog surged in his wake.

"Good morning," Father Jerome said pleasantly as the pilot hooked an arm over the washboard. "If I or my boat can be of any assistance . . ."

"Think you could break us out of this?" He was red-eyed and unshaven; he looked to be, if anything, in worse case than foolish young Chuck-Charley Koskima, who nursed his loganberry hangover in his grandfather's house a mile away.

The priest said dubiously, wishing Chuck-Charley were along to lend his skill, "I'll try. The tide is on the rise, is it not?"

The pilot boarded and hauled his dog after him. "No," he said. "She's dropping. We'll have to move fast."

The dog's vigorous shake sprayed Father Jerome with cold salt water. By the time he had cleared his eyes, the young man had skidded the dinghy off the stern and was sculling across the slough. The girl and the big man in coveralls waded to meet him, trailing the line that ran to

174

the seaplane's tail. He ferried them to the mission boat. They climbed on board. Father Jerome, moving in a flustered dream, started his engine and ran up on his hook.

The pilot's voice jabbed him: "Hurry it, will you?"

With the anchor up and the gasboat's nose pointed down-slough, the pilot threw a figure eight around the stern cleat.

"Try her now," he commanded.

They moved out on a course which would bring the strain directly astern. The line lifted and tightened; the engine labored and the seaplane's tail began to move down the sky. The heels of the floats settled, her nose climbed till she sat level on the bar. The propeller, Father Jerome observed with an anxious eye, was badly bent at either tip.

"Pour it on," the pilot ordered him.

With more of pious hope than expectation, the priest advanced his throttle. Mud boiled under the gasboat's counter. The line vibrated, singing, shedding water in a fine spray. A strand broke with a spiteful pop. But the plane moved, and moved again, sliding smoothly now, off the bar to float free in mid-slough.

The whole business had consumed less than twenty minutes. Father Jerome remembered his errand then, the mission which had brought him from Seahhost in the foggy dawn. He had anticipated a twenty-mile run down the inlet and a further ten miles across open water to the nearest radio-telephone. Perhaps that trip would not be required of him.

He said to the pilot, "Seahhost Village is less than a mile away. I'll tow you there, if you wish."

"Seahhost?" The young man continued to watch his listed plane intently. "I thought only Mounties and the Indian agent ever got into that hole."

"Chief Koskima is a pagan," the priest said quietly, "one of the last. But I believe his humanity will extend to those I sponsor, particularly when they're in trouble."

The dark girl stood with her back to the cabin, the dog leaning against her scratched and mosquito-bitten legs. She said gently, "You've been more than kind to us, Father," and the pilot nodded, accepting Father Jerome's mild reproof.

"We couldn't have made it without you," he said. "I'll get around to thanking you later, sir."

"*Non nobis,*" the little priest said, while his hand lifted in a disclaiming gesture. "Tell me, are you searching for the lost plane?"

"Yes."

"And your name is Ardagh?"

"Yes."

Father Jerome's pale blue eyes misted. He felt, suddenly, that he had been called to move in great events.

"Then you *are* that man, the father who seeks his children. You've had my prayers, Mr. Ardagh, and those of very many others."

"Thanks, Father." The pilot turned, a smile lighting his face briefly, leaving it older with its passing. "Myself, I'm not much good at praying."

It was spoken without cynicism or bravado—humbly, the priest thought. He said, "You believe your children are alive. You search for them. What is that search, Mr. Ardagh, but prayer in action?"

176

This was the true channel; he saw through thinning mist, across a salt-water lagoon, the straggle of frame houses and weathered totem poles, the salmon racks and the slattern gasboats of the Indian village. He said gravely, "I'm one of the least of God's advocates, my son, but I presume to believe He would accept such a prayer as yours. But He might not, in His infinite wisdom, grant it. You must prepare yourself for that."

The outlandish account he had coaxed and bullied from Chuck-Charley Koskima filled his mind again, crowding out theology. If his interpretation of the native boy's experience was correct, his help might extend somewhat farther than hauling a mired seaplane off a bar.

He turned to the pilot; and though his weather-seamed old face remained grave, he could not keep the youthful excitement from his voice.

"I have news for you. It may be of no consequence—you must be the judge. Mr. Ardagh, I'm of the opinion that a boy of Seahhost Village, Charles Koskima, the chief's youngest grandson, not only saw the missing plane immediately before it crashed, but can give you its approximate location."

The pilot's expression did not change. But the fat man sighed and smeared a hand across his face, and the girl moved away from the cabin to stand by the pilot. Father Jerome saw their hands join.

"The night the plane was lost," he said, "this lad was alone in the mountains on a . . . an errand for his grandfather. A plane passed so low over him that it almost swept him from the summit of the ridge where he had intended to spend the night. He tells me it appeared to crash no more than ten miles from that ridge, among the peaks of the Medusa Group at the head of Seahhost Valley."

The priest added half-apologetically, "He was terrified, and attempted to drown his terror in drink. I drew the story from him only last night. I was on my way to report it to the Mounted Police when God blinded my eyes to the channel and diverted me to you."

"Did it burn?" the pilot asked him.

"Chuck-Charley saw no fire. I made a point of asking him. He simply glimpsed the plane through heavy fog, and a few minutes later, heard it crash among the peaks."

The girl said, "Did anyone hear an explosion two nights ago? Or see a glare in the sky?"

"If so, I was not informed." Father Jerome smiled at her, reading, but misinterpreting entirely, the eagerness on the tired and mud-streaked face. "But I'm sure, Mrs. Ardagh, the Indians would have told me had anything untoward been seen or heard."

He glanced at the damaged seaplane towing drunkenly astern and said in a tone of doubt, "I hope your plane can be made serviceable. This boy I've told you of—he's an excellent mechanic. Would new parts be required?"

The big man in the coverall answered him. "Don't know, Padre. I'd say we can brace that buckled strut, and the floats can be patched. One of 'em is pretty badly holed, we ticked a snag when the Captain here made a precautionary landing that wasn't in the book. I'm not sure about the prop, though, and we're out of fuel."

"We can supply gasoline," the priest told him eagerly.

"High octane? It'd need to be over eighty."

178

"Why . . . I'm afraid I can't say." Father Jerome frowned in perplexity, out of his depth as always when faced by a problem of this sort. "I imagine Chuck-Charley will know. It's what the fishermen use in their gasboats."

They were close in now, chugging across the lagoon. "That boy," the priest said, "will think the heavens have opened. He's never had a chance to work on an airplane before. But I very much wish Alex Prince were here. It's a terribly difficult country, inland, and Alex is the only man on the coast who knows the Medusas intimately. He's among them now somewhere, trailing a renegade cougar. Two weeks ago," he said, frowning at the recollection, "the beast showed itself altogether too near the children's swimming pool upriver. Alex wounded it but failed to destroy it."

IN THE YEARS OF HIS SAVAGE PRIME, BEFORE HUNGER AND injury gaunted him, the old tom cougar outweighed a big man. For those touchy seconds while cat and boy confronted each other, the children were in graver danger than they had been at any time since Flight Three rampaged her way down the mountain. Retreat, or any show of panic, might have launched the cougar upon them. The glare and the great explosion had daunted him while he watched Janet from the creek bar with his dull mind all unready still. That night he had found no leftovers from his sons' hunting. When he crouched on the boulder a scant forty feet from the children the next day, he was starving.

The shots left the cougar unharmed, but the noise and the spray of rock chips in his face sent him hightailing up the mountain. He fled, a bad dream given substance, until he was a long way from that meadow, secure in a holt three thousand feet above the Seahhost River forks. That night again, while Alex Prince smoked his pipe in his line cabin at the Forks, the morose old deerslayer tantalized his hunger with a bait of deer mice.

To Don Ardagh, the fear came afterward. Fear crackled through him more briskly than the actual flames among the twigs and punkwood he had managed to gather from windfalls at the edge of the meadow.

Don moved very slowly, with long pauses for rest. The periods of dreaming came oftener; he would stop with a branch in his hand, blankness creeping over his mind like a fog, while his sickly blaze dwindled and threatened to flicker out entirely. During those spells, the fear left him. He stood at the feet of the trees, and the life in him was as slow and stolid as theirs.

Then the fear would jab him, and he would look across the graying meadow toward the boulder which had become terror's lodestone, and work in a small frenzy till the next fit stole upon him.

Most of the wood was damp hereabouts, but into the forest he would not go. Although the watched feeling had gone, it might have betrayed him. And Janet must not be left, must always be in sight.

From the lee of old logs and from windfalls slanting to the pond, he gathered more fuel. Dusk found him still toiling. He had used his last hoarded scraps of waxed paper, and the lighter had caught only after endless clickings. If the fire went out he wouldn't be able to rekindle it.

When his madness of industry waned, he had a reserve pile of limbs and chunks higher than his head, and the fire was rolling out clouds of smoke that fogged the meadow and discouraged even the bloodthirsty mosquitoes. He hunkered down to blow. The crawling flames responded sullenly, steam puffing in tiny jets as they mumbled the wood. Don blew till he was dizzy and sick from smoke.

Behind him, Janet was coughing monotonously. He straightened, the lightheadedness persisting so that he had to set his back against the trunk of the hemlock he had chosen for their shelter. As if the fire had waited only for his ministrations to cease, a flame brightened and lengthened, licking along the underside of a windfall chunk. A beading of pitch caught; in an instant, the fire was live and dancing.

Janet hadn't moved from where he had propped her against the tree bole. She was almost asleep; she snuffled steadily, and her forehead was hot to his touch. The two crusts in his pocket were pulpy from the wet, but he dug them out and tried to feed Janet one. She didn't want to eat it, she only wanted to snuggle up to him and suck her thumb.

It was wrong, her not having milk and cod liver oil and regular meals, but so far she hadn't missed a nap, and last night they'd both had a proper sleep. Her cold bothered him a lot, and he knew wet feet were bad when you had a cold.

He piled the fire higher—he felt at home with fire now, friendly with it and no longer disturbed by the knowledge that he was doing a forbidden thing. The circle of warmth spread, setting their damp clothes to steaming. If they'd had the blankets, this sleeping place would be almost as cozy as the last.

Don brought Janet as close to the fire as he judged safe, peeled her to shirt and diaper, and set about drying her other things. The station-wagon coat was quite dry inside. He spread it on his fuel heap, and pulled out branches to support dress and slip. Sitting with the little girl between his knees, he unlaced her ruined boots and set them to steam with her socks laid over them. Stars were coming out over the pond, and there was only a very little drip from the low-sweeping limbs above them.

He held Janet in his arms, chin on her tangled hair. After a while she stopped shivering. She had long since lost the bandage handkerchief from her hand, and the one from her boot was a sorry rag, but at least it had steamed itself dry enough for him to blow her nose on it.

"Anna," she said in a drowsy croak. "Want Anna."

It was a long time, more than half a day, since she had spoken. He was rejoiced to hear that small voice, even though he couldn't give her what she wanted.

"Anna's gone, baby." His own voice sounded strange in his ears, it was so long since he had used it. "You wait. The picnic will be over soon. Daddy will buy you another Anna."

"Want Anna!" she repeated, squirming and reaching.

182

It was the red hunting cap she wanted. He gave it to her and she hugged it contentedly; the cap, he realized, had taken the place of her lost Teddy bear. He liked the hunting cap a lot, but guessed if it made her happy she could keep it.

As Janet's clothes dried, he put them back on her. After a while the station-wagon coat was finished steaming. He buttoned Janet into it, turned up the fur collar and settled her beside him. Her boots were still wet but the socks were more than dry—one of them had a hole burned in its bottom. Janet had drawn her feet up under the skirts of the wonderful coat. He worked the socks on without waking her.

With his sister looked after, Don took stock of his own clothes. Exertion and the fire had dried him, but his jersey had a three-cornered tear across the chest. Both knees were out of his pants. The stitching had broken in his brown shoes, and the sole of the right one was worn clear through. He guessed he was even dirtier than Janet, and she was grubby enough. But washing faces was too much bother now.

He wasn't hungry. When one of those dreamy fits overtook him, food was no longer part of the dream. Dad was, in a sad kind of way. Don knew that Nora hadn't told Dad after all, and that while he would, of course, find them one day, it didn't have to be tomorrow or even the tomorrow after that.

But as he huddled by the fire, blond head on his knees, his dream was mostly of the blue blankets on the bluff. He wished they had those blankets now. He would make a fine nest with them, heap all the wood on the fire and go to sleep with Janet hugged in his arms. Under the blankets nothing could hurt them. Even if the cougar returned, they'd be safe under the blue blankets.

He thought and thought about the blankets. They would shelter beneath them, safe and snug and warm, not waking, not stirring, until the Viking sat on the pond at last, and they woke with the sun shining and Dad kneeling over them.

The blankets were up on the bluff. The bluff wasn't far —his head was light and his feet were lighter; he could almost float to the place where the blankets lay. The needles-and-pins rhyme began to jingle merrily in his head. He got up, chuckling, and the woods called to him in a voice like Dad's voice, cheerful and kind and strong. The voice lured him from his fire and across the moon-kindled meadow, and up through the shadow cast by the cougar's boulder. The woods were a house and Dad was there and his own feet were on the threshold.

"Donnie!"

Janet's cry pierced that deadly dream and saved him.

She was frightened, she got that way at home sometimes when she wakened and found him gone. Regretfully, he turned from the welcoming woods.

He jogged down past the boulder and back through the marshy meadow that ringed the pond. Janet had cramps in her stomach. He rubbed until the small body ceased to strain, talking to her kindly all the while, and at last she was once more asleep.

He wasn't supposed to sleep. There was a reason why, but it didn't matter now. He piled more wood on the fire and nestled down by Janet, while the fire died, and the meadow cowered beneath the enormous mountain moon.

Then it was daytime again, with rain in the branches and mist-shapes drifting across the wrinkled brown face of the pond. But the night had meshed him in a tangle of dreams, and he could not rid himself of those dreams. There was a black man who had started to tell him a story but didn't get to finish it. There was a dark girl with a kind and pretty face, who ruffled his hair and called him Blondy, and he had pretended to himself that she was his mother. Something had happened to those people, but he couldn't remember what, or where, or when. Try as he would, he couldn't remember.

In the dream, too, there was an unhappy picnic that kept on and on, never going home, with the milk turned sour and the sandwiches growing fewer, a bad animal that snarled at them, and Janet crying because she wanted the picnic to be over.

She wasn't crying now. The mist of dreams parted slowly, and he uncurled from Janet's back and sat up. Automatically, and not realizing for a moment why he did it, Don Ardagh looked across the meadow.

Nothing there. The cougar wasn't watching them, it had not come back.

Lying still, curled around Janet, he hadn't been conscious of the cold. But he felt it now as his damp clothes rasped against his prickling skin, and hugged himself with hands tucked into his armpits as he sat by his sister.

She had cried again in the late night, but between Mother Goose and rubbing her stomach, he had managed to soothe her back to sleep. Gathered into a ball, close to the roots of the tree, she looked like a shot bird lying in a huddle of brown feathers. He slipped a hand under the station-wagon coat. The outside was damp from rain that sifted through the branches in a fine spray, but the inside of the coat was dry and warm. It was almost as good as a little tent, that coat. Last night he had buckled the red hunting cap under her chin, and she hadn't managed to work it loose.

Except for cap and coat, Janet looked very much as she did in her crib, times when he woke first and tiptoed over to see if she needed changing. She wasn't as grown-up a girl as nurse thought she ought to be, and he had learned that the chances of a happy awakening and a posset were better if he changed her before nurse came in.

She was wet now, but he wasn't going to disturb her. There wasn't much to wake up for, he thought with an un-juvenile grimness. Just rain and the ugly brown pond and weeping trees, and the clouds that scudded swiftly in heavy masses overhead. They had nothing to eat, although he didn't care about that any more, and Dad wouldn't come, not on a day like this.

He glanced toward the boulder again, and the boulder was as it had been when last he looked—a smooth hump at the edge of the forest, desolate in the rain.

THEY BEACHED THE VIKING JUST SOUTH OF SEAHHOST VIL-
lage landing. It squatted on log skids now, a battered
and forlorn look about it, the airscrew gone from its nose,
three Indians levering with planks beneath its belly while
Chuck-Charley Koskima swung a sledge against the
buckled strut. His copper torso shone in a drizzle fine
almost as mist; he grinned as he swung.

Brandreth, with a flat stone for an anvil and Ardagh to
help, was straightening the splayed tips of the prop
blades. Jule watched from a drift log. In her persisted the
feeling that this, like the crazy night flight which had
ended so luckily, was part of a dream in which elements
of nightmare remained strong.

It was noon now, the shoulders of her trench coat were
soaked through, but she wouldn't go up to the houses for
all Father Jerome's kindly urging. She wanted desperately
to help with the repair job, and chafed because she could
find nothing at all to do.

Ardagh had been in touch with search base by radio.
Within the hour, three ships had passed, bound in to the
area fixed by the Indian boy. One was an R.C.A.F. plane
—she glimpsed its rondelles clearly before mist swallowed
it. Another was the big U.S. Coast Guard amphibian, and
while she wasn't sure, she believed the third ship which
had come over low with a recognition roll of its silver
wing, was Bill Grady's Fairchild.

She doubted, the way the weather had turned sour again, that they'd be able to do much at the valley head today.

Chuck-Charley was now busy with spruce splints and a coil of wire. He had straightened the strut and was splinting it much as a doctor would immobilize a broken leg. He loved the work; he had spoken hardly a word except for his monosyllabic replies to Ardagh's questions, but his black eyes shone as he toiled at the pilot's bidding.

He ducked out from between the floats. Bare feet planted solidly on the pebbles, he studied the ripped left float. Ardagh came to him and they stood together, the white man a head taller, longer legged, but with a young, eager look to him that matched the boy's.

She would marry him if he wanted her to. That decision, made on the landing at Quartz Harbor, had brought a curious peace with it. But she was still caught in the continuing dream, and the dream would not end till the search was ended.

The boy trotted off to the dock. He returned with a gasoline can. Ardagh nodded, and Chuck-Charley attacked the tin with his sledge, flattening and folding it.

She must have rewound her wrist watch sometime in the night; she glanced at it and another hour had fled away. Brandy had replaced the Viking's propeller and was working on the engine. Father Jerome knelt by the holed float in an attitude of prayer, passing tools to Chuck-Charley.

The drizzle ceased. The air began to hum, and presently the overcast released Grady's seaplane. Grady set down to a neat landing on the lagoon. The tall pilot climbed out at the gasboat floats.

Jule watched nervously as he trudged down the beach. Grady passed her with a dark glance and a shake of his head. He plodded through loose shingle toward the Viking. Jule got up from the log, her apprehension deepening, and tagged after him.

But Grady said nothing to Ardagh of last night's adventure. He merely stood by the patched seaplane, eyeing it dubiously.

Jule thought, *They haven't found anything yet. He wouldn't act like this if they had.*

Grady said, "The Medusas are socked in solid. Nobody's found a hole yet, Vince. Thought I'd look in and see how you were doing."

"We've got her made, just about," Ardagh said. He straightened, and his voice and face revealed no more than the search chief's. "What's doing down at Quartz?"

"I had a signal for you," Grady said. "A love note from Inspector Langmuir." His tone was still casual, his rocky face blank. "Seems like I've lost it, though."

He lit a cigarette and trickled smoke from his nose while he studied the weather up toward the valley head. "Nothing big enough in yonder for us to set down on," he said. "I'm going to base the Grumman and the R.C.A.F. recce ship here. I hauled up a few spare drums for them."

Grady turned, smiling, to the little priest. "Father, excuse me. I didn't recognize you, messed up like you are. Last time we met, you were doing some overdue marrying at Tamahous Arm. You think you could round up a few parishioners and help me unload?"

His smile widened to a grin. "I've got to get back downcoast and rig a ground party. By the way, this man here isn't supposed to take off till he gets his certificate of airworthiness reinstated. Watch him. He might just try to tap those fuel drums."

Father Jerome peered shortsightedly at Grady, and what he read on the search captain's face brought a relieved smile to his lips.

"I'm not entirely trustworthy," he said. "In fact I might even compound a felony, if it happened to be on the side of the angels."

When Grady lifted his Fairchild off the lagoon, three red drums of aviation fuel sat on the landing. Brandreth tinkered another half-hour. Finally he climbed down heavily to the beach.

"I wouldn't want to be your insurance agent," he said, "but she may do, Captain. She may just do."

Ardagh squatted to give the splinted strut a critical inspection. It seemed to Jule that the tension which had left him for a while there, had returned. He said, "If that kid had only gone in. If he'd even got to a phone ..."

He shook his head, the old look taking the life from his face, hardening him again.

"He helped us," Jule said. "He helped a lot, Vince. Be grateful for that. And if someone was alive two nights ago, they may be still. It's a better chance than we started with, isn't it?"

It seemed to Jule that the entire population of Seahhost must be on the beach. Men, women, and the same swarm of black-eyed children who had watched the work, crowded the foreshore. A very old man stood apart. Like a shawl over his shoulders he wore a goat's-hair blanket patterned with abalone shell, a blanket such as Jule had seen previously only behind museum glass. His dignity was immense; he had a severe, rather fine face, and when Father Jerome addressed him, it was with obvious respect.

The clucking exchange ended. The priest crossed to them. He said, "Chief Koskima doesn't expect the weather to change, Mr. Ardagh. He asks if you feel it wise to proceed."

"She may clear," Ardagh answered stubbornly. "Thank him for us, Father. Tell him if they ever need anyone flown out, to send for me." The tide was lapping against the lowest of the drift skids on which the Viking rested. "I think we can launch now," he said.

The seaplane took the water easily. She floated in balance again, looking jaunty and buoyant against the cloud-dulled green of the lagoon. Ardagh stood on a float deck with a pikepole while a swarm of boys in two dilapidated dugout canoes towed the Viking to the dock where the fuel drums waited in a row.

It was two-fifteen by Jule's watch when Ardagh signaled Chuck-Charley to stop pumping. He called to Brandreth, "No belly tanks. I want to keep her light. . . . What do you think you're doing, Brandy?"

"Going with you," Brandreth said. He mounted to the cabin. "You're not flying that light, Captain. In back, there ain't any siwash mechanics to help if you get stuck."

Jule got in, too. Tagish scrambled to his place on the heap of tarpaulins aft of the cockpit seats. Ardagh swung in behind the wheel. He said to Jule in an impersonal voice, "Fasten that belt this time, eh?"

The engine caught, the sputtering discords partly smoothed as the pilot warmed her. They taxied out from the landing. Father Jerome, beside the old chief, raised his hand in a salute which was half farewell, half blessing. The seaplane turned into the wind, the roar became deafening, the huddled houses of the village were flashing past. Three-quarters of the way down the lagoon, with the salt flats rushing toward them, the Viking rose on her steps.

Jule hadn't expected it to fly; and she knew Brandreth was worried under his calm. To her the repair job had seemed crude and unorthodox. She held her breath, seeing the houses grow smaller and the people on the landing diminish to doll size as the plane banked and climbed northeast up the valley trough.

The mountains were smothered, their ragged crests did not break through the lowering clouds. But the Medusa peaks were in there, waiting, and the knowledge sent a cold ripple along Jule's spine.

THE GRAY AND MIZZLING DAY WAS WELL ALONG WHEN IN the course of his traverse from the den above the Seahhost Forks, the old tom cougar followed his nose to the bluff where Don Ardagh had left the blankets. He should have been sleeping, not hunting. But deer mice were poor fare for a carnivore who could devour a blacktail doe at two sittings, and hunger and wounds had conspired to turn the one-eyed cat's world upside down.

The hateful, intriguing and now-familiar scent was cold, but he approached cautiously against the wind, shadowing from the timber only when ears and eye confirmed his nose in its report that the bluff was untenanted.

He circled the blankets, tail tip twitching gently. Satisfied with his inspection at last, he poked at the blanket tangle with a tentative paw. There was no loud explosion, no pain across his shoulders or sudden stinging of his face.

The cougar hooked again at the tangle—bolder now—caution and ingrained fear of man retreating as the half-expected reprisal did not come. His claws snagged in the wool, and fear did touch him for an instant, but the blanket tore and released him. He pounced on the bundle then, ripping and tossing it, shredding the blankets in a parody of kittenish play.

But his mood was not kittenish, and the blankets offered nothing to stay his hunger. For a long time he squatted amid the litter he had made, conning the woods below with nose and stub ears and single slitted yellow eye. The cold trail did not end here. The creatures who owned that scent were below, in the deer's twilight meadow in the valley.

The race caution stirred in him, but only weakly. That unplayful frolic with the blankets had dealt caution a mortal blow. He sat a while longer with his hate and his aches and his hunger pains. Then, purposefully, he flowed down from the bluff and resumed his soundless ghosting through the forest.

Across the mountain, old Alex Prince stood among his pack with his rifle in the crook of his arm, cursing each several hound and crossbreed exhaustively by name.

193

They had picked up scent not half an hour from the cabin, circled with it through bottomland choked with rank devil's club, then their village-dulled noses had lost it here on a sand bar not ten minutes from the Forks.

The track before him was not that of the cat Alex hunted. A much smaller beast, one of the renegade's sons, had left these prints from which the stocky Indian turned now with a grunt of disgust.

Alex cut and trimmed an alder gad while his dogs watched with an apprehensive sliding of eyes. They scattered as he waded into them, but he landed licks enough to raise a chorus of yelps and to lighten his own spleen. When the tumult subsided, Alex hazed them across the shallow-flowing east fork and up the near-precipitous slope opposite.

The one-eyed cat had always ranged high. Up yonder, close to timberline at the four-thousand-foot level, they'd have a better chance of cutting his trail.

His mood was dour. For many years the Medusa bowl had been his private reserve. White men kept out of it. But today two airplanes had passed over already, and the mountain silence which had been balm to his ears after the clacking of village voices was being invaded again.

This third plane flew lower than the others, and its engine sounded rougher. From the gut of a steep and brushy draw, Alex watched it roar over, yellow beneath the threatening clouds that packed the Medusas solid from peaks to timberline. Those damned machines would scare everything out of the country.

He watched the seaplane disappear, grumpily wondering whether he should call off his hunt. A man was seven kinds of fool to go after cougar before the first snowfall, anyhow. But from the rock castles above the sidehill rim, his pack leader began to holler in the hysteria of a new find, and Alex resumed his toilsome progress up the draw.

Men afoot in mountain country reckon travel not by the mile but by the hour. Alex Prince was then two hours of hard bushwhacking from the pond in the northeast corner of the old cat's range. While he chivvied his pack away from the mouth of the holt above the Forks, the one-eyed cougar was drifting with the mist of the gray day, down toward the mossy bluff where three blue blankets lay soaking in the rain.

TWICE, AT FIVE HUNDRED FEET, ARDAGH DRAGGED THE WILD valley. It was very heavily forested. The only breaks were where rock outcrops broke through, or where one or other of the tiny ponds scarred the great, dark sprawling hide of the timber. The ponds were mere puddles. Not one of them offered room to slideslip a float plane down, let alone get it off again. A lake twenty miles north in the next valley was the nearest feasible spot for a landing.

He was not concerned with the valleys, though. The area which he had to cover, untouched yet in the search, lay higher. But that sector below the peaks remained stubbornly cloudfast, as it had yesterday and this morning when the other ships from Quartz Harbor attempted to probe it.

He ought to set down on the lake, wait for a possible break instead of squandering gas like a fool. But the afternoon was passing—it was three o'clock now, and on this gray day dusk would settle early. In any case, he should unload Jule and Brandy before undertaking what might be a very dangerous venture. Still, he needed their eyes. If he did find a hole through which he could drop the Viking, the period of contact would be brief.

There was no point in telling them what he proposed to do. Brandy would guess as soon as they began to climb; and tough-nerved as Jule had shown herself, it might be better if she didn't know.

He glanced once over his shoulder as he started the Viking upstairs. Brandy, knee on a jump seat, was hunched by the forward cabin window, peering down. Jule sat much as Nora had, turned from him, forearm on the right-hand window sill, chin on wrist. He had scarcely thought of Nora since he unloaded her at Quartz Harbor yesterday, and she entered his mind only glancingly now. He could count on Jule, always and completely. Scared she might be, but she wouldn't betray him.

On his map Mount Medusa, the kingpin of the range, showed as just over eight thousand feet. He lifted the seaplane out of the valley, losing contact at four thousand, climbing through blinding murk. At a little over eighty-five hundred, they broke through to clear sky. Cloud lay solid below, piled against the summits from northern to southern horizon. But the cloud plain was not level. Where the taller peaks rose, columns of vapor boiled and churned, thrusting over the plain like pillars of a ruined and roofless temple in the sky.

He banked the Viking, setting course for the area where the vapor boiled most turbulently over the masked summits. That cauldron, he knew, marked the arc of peaks which comprised the Medusa group. It was a place to shun, a hot spot such as he would have given a wide berth to in normal flight. But he had tossed Air Regulations into the discard long past. It was there and only there, amid these shipwrecking drafts and eddies, that the hole he needed might open.

The area of turbulence was close now. He had tested his prop control and the rough landing hadn't damaged it —the blades still responded. He flattened them for utmost power, opened the throttle, and with a glance to assure himself that Jule's belt was tight-cinched, hurled the Viking into that aerial tide rip.

They were tossed and buffeted. A downdraft snatched at the starboard wing tip. Ardagh fought the Viking out of her spin, seeing a hole like an inverted funnel, seeing through the hole the darker gray of mountain rock, the dirty white of snow rushing up at them. He levelled at a hundred feet. The seaplane dragged that tilted snowfield hanging on her prop. Down-mountain, mist coiled over long slopes, splintered terraces, gullies and avalanche troughs. His own eyes found nothing of what they sought. But Jule had turned from the window with her hand stabbing down, and Brandy's fist was pounding his shoulder.

He banked, keyed for the first warning flutter of a stalled wing, pulled on the throttle knob, and scoured the field below the peak recklessly again, straining to see what those two had seen in the remnant of winter's snow.

In that first veiled glimpse, Jule had thought it no more than a boulder strangely isolated there. It was not till the fog had closed that her mind weighed and evaluated the evidence of her eyes.

Brandreth had spotted it too—he was behind Ardagh, leaning on the back of the seat, shouting in the pilot's ear: *"Her tail section! Chunk of her wing!"*

On their second sweep across the field, Jule saw those tokens of disaster clearly. The duralumin fin knifed out of the snow. Beyond it on the soiled white, the broken wing section lay half-buried, tipped on edge by the weight of the two engines.

The Viking was weaving across the lower slopes now with staccato throttle bursts in powered glide and bank and glide. The fog was tattering. Jule saw a gash on the mountain's shoulder darker than the rest. She pointed, horror swamping the blaze of triumph, turning her voiceless as they swept low over the gully.

Hurricane had struck here with fire for aftermath. She saw tree stumps charred and blackened, flame-dulled dural scattered in shards and rolls and twisted grotesqueries of tormented metal. The nose and flight deck sat apart, near the foot of the shallow gully. That portion of the plane was scorched but recognizable. It seemed to have escaped the full force of the explosion that reddened the sky two nights earlier.

She was looking down at the blasted and dismembered carcass of Coastwise-Pacific Airlines' Flight Three from Los Angeles, the four-engined ship that had hurtled out of fog and into the fog again, that had gone lost and wandering to her death on a dark mountain three hundred miles from port.

The gully was astern, the Viking was lifting toward the overcast. Jule looked at Ardagh with a dreadful sinking of her heart. But the pilot's face was oddly serene, and his square, blunt-fingered hands were steady on the wheel. They were climbing, bearing in toward the peak again. Something struck the Viking a hammer blow, so that she lurched and staggered in the air. There were two other blows, and while the plane still shuddered from the impact, the engine died. The dark north face leaped at them, the snowfield rushed toward them. Left wing down, fuselage shoving against air, the Viking slanted toward the snow. The wing tip rose, and Ardagh hauled back on the steering column in the instant before the floats struck. A grinding crash shook the plane. Sight was obscured by a white wave driving in over the airscrew as she churned up the slope.

Without transition, it seemed to Jule, the Viking lost her forward way and began to glide backwards, smoothly, in an echoing silence. She felt cold air on her neck, turned to see Brandreth launch himself through the cabin doorway in a clumsy leap.

Ardagh ripped at her safety belt. His other hand flung open the door. There was a check in the smooth and silent descent, and he shoved her violently out. She rolled, banging her head, spinning over and over till a hand closed on her wrist and checked her.

They sprawled on a corrugated apron of dark-blue ice, Brandreth below, Ardagh against him, still gripping her wrist. Of the Viking, Jule saw no sign. Twenty feet down-slope from Brandreth, the ice-apron dipped to air. Above, the edge of the snowfield showed sharp as if cut by a knife.

"You first," Ardagh said. "Across to the rock. Take it easy—the rest may come down."

On hands and knees, Jule crawled across the apron to the rock spur at the base of the peak. Ardagh and Brandreth followed her. Something black moved in the snow above the avalanche break. Tagish crossed to them with a swimming motion, only his prick-eared head clear.

"What happened?" Jule asked.

"Cylinder let go," Brandreth said. And calmly to Ardagh, as he fished for his tobacco pouch, "Captain, next time suppose you pick one that ain't got ice under it. All she needed was the smack we gave her to start sliding."

Ardagh said gruffly, "If you hadn't stopped her, we'd have gone over with her, Brandy. How'd you do it?"

"Got myself in the way of a float," Brandreth said, his little eyes grinning at Jule between their pouches of flesh. "She countersunk me right into the ice." He twisted the ends of a brown-paper cigarette and stuck it between his lips. "Sometimes it don't hurt to have a fat man along."

The rock rib offered a line of descent to the first of the crumbled terraces. They moved out in single file from the shadow of the peak. A thousand feet down the mountain, they could see the gully's fire-blackened gash.

IF IT WERE JUST HIM, DON ARDAGH THOUGHT, HE WOULD have been content to sit with his back against the tree and let his dreams take him completely. But Janet was going to wake sometime, and when she did, it would be better if there was a fire.

His fire of the night before had burned out. The branches he had dragged from the windfalls across the pond poked blackened butts into the circle of ash. He broke off twigs, made a tent of them, and clicked the cigarette lighter. The flame was puny, and before the twigs could catch, it went out. He couldn't coax another flame in spite of repeated clickings. After a while the lighter even stopped throwing sparks.

Don got up from his knees, letting the lighter drop unheeded among the ashes. They were going to miss the fire. The long picnic hadn't seemed so bad when they had that dance of flames to warm and dry and cheer them.

He had no plan for the day. Reaching the pond had been his only goal. They had reached it, but the Viking hadn't landed after all, and the pond and its bordering meadow had become the limit of the little boy's world. Somewhere a tremendous distance beyond, memory told him vaguely, lay the ocean. But in a million years they couldn't travel that far, not with Janet having to be carried most of the way.

Dad had read him a story about a wolf-boy once, far

201

back in another, happier life. The story had scared him, but pleasantly, the way you could let yourself be scared in a cozy house at night. That's what they were now, he thought. Wolf-children, living under a tree. But the boy in the story had friends among the animals, and from what he had seen of the cougar, he doubted if it was an animal you could make friends with.

He looked toward the boulder again, not expecting to see the cougar because he hadn't been warned by the feeling that prickled the back of his neck when it was around. The gun someone had given him in a long-ago dream was no more use; but maybe pointing it would scare the cougar away, if he did return.

The smooth hump of the boulder remained unbroken. Don started to walk to the pond for a drink. But his legs played tricks on him, and after he had fallen twice, he decided it would be easier to go without the drink for a while. He rested where he had last tumbled, then when his head stopped spinning, got up and moved slowly back to the ashes of the fire. The day was a lot darker than it should be for morning. He pondered the fact, wondering how long he had slept, staring down at the ashes.

Their fire hadn't been entirely friendly. Sometime in the night—Don guessed it was after he had got up to pile the last of the wood on it—the flames had licked out to Janet's boots. The toe was burned out of one white boot, and when he took the other in his hands, the leather was stiff and brittle.

Janet was stirring; in a minute she'd open her eyes and smile at him. Then she'd ask for a posset. The thought pierced his dullness with an aching hurt. He felt like crying, but he didn't seem to have anything left to cry with.

But when Janet woke, she didn't ask for a posset. Instead she said in her husky, croaking little voice, parroting her brother as she so often did, "The doggy won't hurt you. The nice doggy won't hurt you."

There had been no warning, no cold and sudden tingle that told of watching eyes. He turned, slowly, not wanting to face the boulder across the meadow, but drawn as if a hand swung him by the shoulder.

The cougar had come back. It sat on top of the boulder, a wicked and ugly creature left over from the dream tangles of the night. It looked like a great tawny cat up there, and it watched them with the same fixed interest Nora's cat showed when it studied the houseboy's talking mynah bird.

"You lie down, baby," Don said. "You go back to sleep."

Moving his hand very slowly, he worked the gun from his pocket. Even without bullets, it might scare the cougar away.

He pointed the gun as he had the day before, holding it in both hands, his face set in a scowl. The cougar didn't move. Don pointed till his arms shook with weariness; and as the gun sagged, its weight and his arms' exhaustion bringing it down, the cat shape changed, flattening and lengthening.

It seemed to flow rather than drop from the boulder. The bushes screened it, but he could see their tops shivering, marking its silent course along the tongue of scrub. The cougar emerged to the meadow's edge. In grass that reached to its shoulders, it paused with lifted head. The Halloween mask turned full upon them, wrinkling into a grin. Then the cougar began to flow across the meadow.

Don dropped the gun. Among the half-burned branches was a limb longer than he was tall. He stooped for it and raised it in a tight, two-fisted grip. Feet planted wide, the ashes of the fire before him and Janet sucking her thumb in the shelter of his braced legs, he waited.

There was a point beyond fear. You came to it only when you had been terribly afraid for a very long time. Then something broke inside you, and you didn't feel much of fear or hope or anything any more. He knew only, with a complete lack of emotion, that the cougar must not get past him.

It was most of the way across the meadow now, its shoulders moving steadily above the marsh grass, the one eye of the grinning mask fixed upon him. He gripped the charred limb tighter, and stepped away from Janet, across the ashes, toward the cougar.

Movement flashed in his eye-corner. A black shape drove past the boulder and into the brush. The meadow grass rippled as if a sudden arrow of wind rushed down from the mountain. The cougar was out of the marsh and advancing with a dainty stepping. But Don stared past it, seeing that swift ripple slash the meadow, hearing over the whisper of cleft grass an unimportant sound, a metallic chinking, the jingle of a dog tag against a studded collar.

He saw the great black-and-tan dog explode from the wild hay.

He heard his own voice screaming, *"Tagish! Tagish!"*

204

THE GULLY TOLD THEM NO MORE AND NO LESS THAN ARDAGH had expected to learn. He stood on the rim beside Jule and Brandreth now, while Tagish ranged somewhere among the jumbled rocks below.

When a board of inquiry sat, Ardagh knew approximately what its basic findings would be. Flying on three engines, unable to outclimb the weather, off course and out of radio contact, she had roved blind until the mountain reached for her. By the wreckage on the avalanche slope above, she had struck first at the six-thousand-foot level, driving in through the north pass and tearing her tail and fire-gnawed wing off against the shoulder of the rock peak.

"Bears was around," Brandreth said. "I found a dead one." His large face was pasty, and he was striking match after match without getting a light for his cigarette. "I guess maybe bears started the fire, Captain, knocking around."

Ardagh nodded. His mind worked coldly as he jogged down in the direction Tagish had taken.

This was the end of it. They had found the lost one and got their answer, and there was no further use or reason for belief. He had held two tickets in a rigged draw, one on a boy who loved him and whom he loved, the other on a little girl whom he had also loved, but who wouldn't likely have remembered him if they'd landed safe from Flight Three. It was over now. He could tear up his tickets.

Tagish barked from below, among the rocks. Ardagh trudged down to the boulder field, a man without hope; and the dog was waiting for him there, sitting by a cleft between two in-leaning boulders. A freak of the crash had dropped a dural sheet like a hearth before it.

Tagish whined, deep in his throat.

"Come on," the pilot said to him. "Nothing for us here."

But the Doberman snuffed at the cleft; then, whining still, padded to the shallow creek that spread itself among the rocks.

Jule and Brandy had followed him from above. Jule said in a voice so low it was almost a whisper, "He's found something, Vince."

Ardagh stepped away from the cleft. He said, "What is it, mister? What are you trying to tell us?"

The big, lean dog moved on along the creek bed, picking his way carefully. He rustled into brush, not whining now, working steadily downstream until the tangles hid him from their sight.

Brandreth said in a quiet voice, "Look at this."

He held a green thermos jug, dripping from the creek. A neat round hole was punched through its belly.

Bullet hole or freak of the explosion, Ardagh couldn't be sure which. But he turned abruptly away, seeing the Doberman burst from the creek-bottom thickets and strike north toward the head of an old rock slide on which alpine hemlock grew sparsely among the slabs. Tagish barked to him again, but did not wait. As Ardagh started down toward him, the dog began to pick his way along the slide.

Ardagh descended the creek at half a run, the brush popping and crackling as he smashed through. Before he had gained the top of the slide, Tagish was barking again to him from its foot, three hundred yards down-mountain. This was a different, excitement-roughened kind of bark, an imperative and triumphant summons.

Loose rock skidding and rolling under his boots, Ardagh plunged on down toward the creek's next bend and the parkline stand of large trees that marked true timberline. The dog stood in a cove made by the roots of a giant hemlock. Those roots were ridged like knuckles, the thin soil eroded around them by a succession of freshets. Tagish snuffed at something which trailed from one of the lesser roots. His tail stirred gently, and the whine rumbled in his chest again.

The thing was the belt of a child's coat, secured around the root with three half-hitches. The other end, the buckle end, formed a noose. Close by were the sodden remains of a campfire.

Staring down, Ardagh saw four pebbles balanced one upon another, and ringing them in an orderly pattern like the petals of a daisy, a circle of evergreen cones.

His brain which had so coldly reconstructed cause and effect in Flight Three's death, now stumbled in a daze, shying away from the truth his eyes revealed to him. Then joy in a great stinging flood surged through him, and he dropped a hand to the Doberman's neck, gathering the loose hide, roughing Tagish behind the ears till the whine became a whimper of protest.

They were alive. They had got this far alive.

Tagish moved out from under his hand. His muzzle lifted in a careful, dubious testing of the air. He crossed to the bar and whined again there, but with no stirring of his tail. Striding toward him, Ardagh saw the hair stiffen and rise on the Doberman's shoulders as he forded the shrunken creek.

Rain had blurred the prints, but they retained enough of their round and scalloped shape to tell the story. They were old tracks—days old. Two days ago, or three, a very large cougar had stood here.

Tagish looked up at him, the whine half a growl, and Ardagh said to him sharply, "Go on. Don't wait for me. Find 'em!"

The cat didn't have to be trailing them. It might have come out to the bar before or after the children paused here. Ardagh forced his mind into the near-trancelike state of suspension again. The creek jungles had held Jule and Brandy up. He glimpsed them, silhouetted against the clearing sky at the top of the rock slide, as he hurried down through the woods after Tagish.

Presently the timber opened to a low bluff, one of those outcrops that broke the flow of the forest. He saw blue shreds and tatters on the scuffed moss, and approached slowly, in sickness and great dread. But there was nothing here to stay him, and the dog was ranging somewhere on below.

They must have traveled very slowly. A boy of eight packing blankets and shepherding a small child would be lucky to make a quarter of a mile in an hour. Ardagh judged that the children had reached this point in their fantastic journey sometime yesterday. The blankets puzzled him—having brought them this far, why would Don abandon them when the going below was so much easier?

They must have had food. Without food, it was unlikely they would have struggled this distance on what he now felt was a purposeful trek toward the valley. Then what had happened here? Food gone, maybe. Strength ebbing. Of one thing he was now certain—the cat had been trailing them, and with malice.

A carbine in the tail compartment of a seaplane piled under a cliff was no use to him here. He didn't even have a pocket knife. At the next windfall, Ardagh leaned his weight on a butt limb, heaving and wrenching till it cracked. He twisted it loose from the trunk, snapped the thin end over his knee, and followed on after Tagish.

From above he had seen a pond and a scrap of meadow pocketed at valley head. They'd been traveling toward the pond.

It was nearer than he had thought. In something under five minutes, he caught the pewter shine of the pond through the trees. A boulder humped from the easy slope ahead. He skirted it; and hip-deep in blueberry scrub, looked across the crescent meadow. He saw boy and cougar, and the dog rushing in.

The cougar wheeled, and in wheeling was bowled clear off its feet by the Doberman's charge. It rolled at the meadow's edge with a flourish of paws. While it still clawed air, Tagish rushed it again. The beast squalled in fury and in pain. As it righted itself, Ardagh glimpsed the red rip across its shoulder where the dog had slashed.

The meadow was boggy, it clutched hard at his feet, sinking him boot-top deep at every lunging stride. The cat squatted now, pivoting as Tagish circled. The dog's snarl made steady thunder; the cougar, after that single squall, faced its adversary in deadly quiet.

Ardagh, still bogged, still plowing toward them, saw Tagish break his wolfish circling. The Doberman feinted, dodged from a lashing paw, and feinted again. The cougar hooked at him and the dog darted in, low and rocket-fast, over the grappling forearm. There was a confused and flashing flurry. Then a taloned paw caught Tagish and whirled him end over end into the meadow.

Ardagh shouted. He broke from the prisoning mud, and the cougar spun to front him. Its torn mask dripped blood. It crouched with swishing tail and backward-flattened ears, the humped shoulders settling, the whole gaunt body contracting. Beyond it, across the ashes of a dead fire, the boy stood as if frozen, a charred stick in his hands.

The cougar's head moved from side to side with a snakelike weaving. The beast hissed too, like a snake. Ardagh ran in upon it, and while the spring was still building, struck down two-handed at that hissing mask. The blow skidded. He lurched aside as a paw flailed at his knee. A sudden tumult of dogs' voices broke around him. He saw their milling shapes as he struck again. A human voice roared at him, but he raised the hemlock club and chopped down once more with all his might across the cougar's back.

A hand clamped on his shoulder and yanked him away.

The voice bellowed in his ear, "You want to get yourself killed?"

The old tom cougar propped himself in a ring of dogs who for all their frantic threats maintained a careful distance. Alex Prince, sane in a world gone mad, brooded thirty feet away with his rifle laid over his arm.

He was a stolid man, but the thing that made him love these mountains stirred in him now, so that he felt toward the broken beast a queer surge of pity and regret. He very much doubted that its intention had been to attack the crazy white man who had dropped out of nowhere. His dog had blinded its one good eye, it had been trying to escape him, and he had smashed its back.

"You old devil," Alex Prince said softly. *"You mis'able old devil."* In a gesture of casual grace, he swung the Enfield to his shoulder, sighted and squeezed the trigger.

When he turned, the fair-haired man was on his knees in the ashes of a cold fire, weeping while he hugged two ragged and very dirty children in his arms.

Tagish limped up from the meadow. Parallel across his side were five red claw-gashes. The cougar pack paused in their maul to bristle at the stranger, but he passed them with no more than a lifting of his lip. He strode to the children and the kneeling man, and his tail waved gently as he sniffed at the little boy's face.

MIDNIGHT WAS LONG PAST WHEN JULE CASED HER PORTABLE. The radio-telephone operator sagged in his chair, snoring gently. Rick Hyatt had mooched out some time ago, grumbling about the pictures he had missed, but, Jule knew, more pleased at the outcome of the search than he was ever likely to admit.

Brandreth sat with his feet cocked on the table that had held Bill Grady's maps.

"Finished?" he asked.

"And about time," Jule said. She tapped the sheets of her story together. It would be page one with a twelve-point byline. McDevitt had promised her that, and his apology had been downright courtly.

"If I had Pilate's bowl, Miss Thorne," he had told her, "I would at this moment break it over my head."

A smile tugged at her lips. She and Vince would need every cent they could scrape together—she wondered whether Mac's gratitude would run to a raise.

"You know," Brandreth said, "I've been thinking, Jule. I think I'll go back to work for the Captain. They overpay me where I'm at, and I've got a few bucks saved."

"But you told me he wouldn't let you work for nothing."

"That wouldn't be for long. There'll be no stopping him now." The big man stared at his muddy boots on the table. "You ready to tell me why yet, kid?"

"You know why, Brandy."

"A good thing," he said. "A good thing." He yawned hugely, and said with his eyes screwed shut, "He's still over there at the hospital, fussing and fretting. If your homework's done, you could drop by."

She was bone-weary, but she went out lightly, smiling still, and crossed the street and walked down it toward the little Red Cross Outpost Hospital on the Point. In the hours since the helicopter had relayed them down from the meadow to Seahhost where the Coast Guard amphibian waited, her happiness had settled into a profound and quiet content. Janet had come ashore in her arms, and the solemn blond boy had let her kiss him good night. From Don, she felt, that was a major concession.

Tagish met her at the foot of the hospital steps and convoyed her in his dignified fashion to the door. Ardagh was there, hunched in a chair with his chin propped on his fists.

The children had started the night with a bed each, but while she was away writing her story, Don must have wakened and climbed in with Janet. As she crossed to them now, she saw in dim outline the two heads nestled on one pillow.

"How are they?" she asked Ardagh.

"Doing fine." He got up quietly, and went to fetch her a chair from over by the window. "They've both got colds. Janet has a sprained thumb. Barring mosquito bites and bruises, Doc Bernstein can't find much else wrong with them."

"Did Don talk?" That had worried her most of all. The boy had uttered hardly a word about the crash, or their days and nights alone on the mountain.

"He came unstuck. I think I've got most of it now."
Ardagh leaned forward to settle the covers closer around
his son's shoulders. "Some parts he's forgotten. Bernstein
says he doesn't want to remember them, and may not for
a long time. It's better that way."

"Much better," Jule agreed, and Ardagh smiled at her,
making her feel strange with him suddenly, flustered and
shy as a young girl.

He said to her, "What do you think of them?"

"Two sweet children," Jule said. "They look a lot like
their pictures."

"Brandy likes them. You'd never guess it, but he has a
way with kids."

After a while Jule said, "Speaking of pictures, Rick
Hyatt was talking to me about the one Connor tried to
stop him from taking. The one on the dock."

"Uh-huh." He didn't sound particularly interested.
"Hyatt shouldn't have taken it."

He recalled the look on Don's face as Nora broke out
of the mob on Quartz Harbor landing and tried to gather
him into her arms—that glare of hatred and loathing, and
the hands like claws that rose to fend Nora away.

"You remember I told you Nora knocked herself out.
We flew over them yesterday, close over. I'd counted on
her to spot on the right-hand side. Don saw her. He's
got it fixed in his head she spotted them and didn't tell
me."

Jule considered that, studying the two small, peaceful
faces.

"He shouldn't feel so about his mother."

"She isn't his mother." Ardagh spoke quietly, but with

214

something of the old, unyielding dourness in his voice. "I've talked to her, Jule. I let her take them once, because I thought someday she'd come back. She'll never have them again. They aren't hers now. And she doesn't want them, I don't believe she ever did, not the way kids have to be wanted. All Nora cares about is getting south again, out of here."

"Rick Hyatt means to give you that negative," Jule told him. "He says no judge in the country would take them from you when he saw that." They were hers now, too; she meant to protect them. "I think you'd better keep it, Vince."

Don's head stirred on the pillow. His eyes opened.

"Everything's okay," Ardagh said to him gently. "We're here."

"I'm hungry."

"No more for a while," Ardagh said. "You can have a gallon of milk and two dozen eggs in the morning, both of you."

"Isn't it morning yet, Dad?"

"No, you dope." The gruff voice brought the smile to Jule's mouth again. She had seen how he nursed the blond head against the chest of his greasy flight jacket coming down, and the tear runnels on his face. "You go to sleep."

"I can't. I want to know the rest of the story."

"What story?"

"About a boy called Pana . . . Pan . . . A funny name."

"Apanamondas," Jule said.

"Yes. His aunty gave him a puppy dog and he cooled it in the water on a leaf." Don sat up and wrapped his

215

arms around his knees. "What did he do with the loaf of bread?"

"He dragged it home on a string," Jule said. "It's a long story, Don. I'll tell you all of it in the morning."

"I want to know how it ended." He was watching her; his face was shadowed, but she knew he was smiling at her. "Please, Jule?"

"It ends with pies," she said. "His mammy made two persimmon pies, and she set them on the doorstep to cool. ' 'Panamondas,' she told him, 'Now you just be careful how you steps on my persimmon pies, you hear me?' " Her heart sang, and laughter bubbled in her voice. "And 'Panamondas was real careful, Don. He stepped right in the middle of each of them!"

Don settled back to sleep. They were quiet a long time. Then Ardagh said to her, "What about you, Jule?"

"I got my job back, if that's what you mean. You'll hate me when you see tomorrow's paper."

"No," he said. "No, I won't hate you." He got up and reached for her hands. "I want you around. It's a long chance, Jule. A lot of rough going. But I wish you'd take it."

"I want to take it," she said, and he kissed her then, but not as he had in the radio shack.

They stood looking down at the children. Ardagh said softly, "They weren't the only lost ones. I was lost. I guess you were too."

"That's over," Jule said, in the quiet dark, his arm around her. "We aren't lost now, Vince. We won't be, any more."